LAKSHMANA'S LAST STAND

THE RISE OF NAGVANSHIS

RAJ THAMBU

INDIA · SINGAPORE · MALAYSIA

ISBN
Paperback 979-8-89475-988-3
Hardcase 979-8-89519-520-8

Preface

Listen, ye Lakshmana! my brother, and my conscience keeper, listen to this!

In my dreams, I see uncanny visions of a raging battle against an eternal evil

For we do not know the nameless worlds we cross, the countless fights we wage in forgotten epochs

With each evil defeated in the bygone era, cometh a new darker evil that posits a starker challenge

With each war bigger, and each stake higher, yet my purpose remains.

Know, ye Sesha! you of a pure mind, and a brave heart, know this!

My arrow is but one, yet it fuses the head, the rod, and the tail

My soul is but one, yet it lives to protect my Saketa, Samaja, and Samsara

My path is but one, yet it guides me to discharge my duty and my purpose.

Feel, ye Anuja! my shadow, the reflection of my soul, feel this!

All that we saw, all that we experienced, all that we overcame is not the end

For what is happening has already happened, and what has happened will happen again.

Just as we prevailed in previous yugas, we shall yet return in the next, to battle that evil

In this, I will not rest until time ends or until Adharma ends!

This is my Samhita. And this is Ram Rajya!

In loving memory of

my late mother

Smt. Padmavathy

Prologue

More than two decades have passed since the decisive battle in Lanka, with Rama firmly establishing a rule

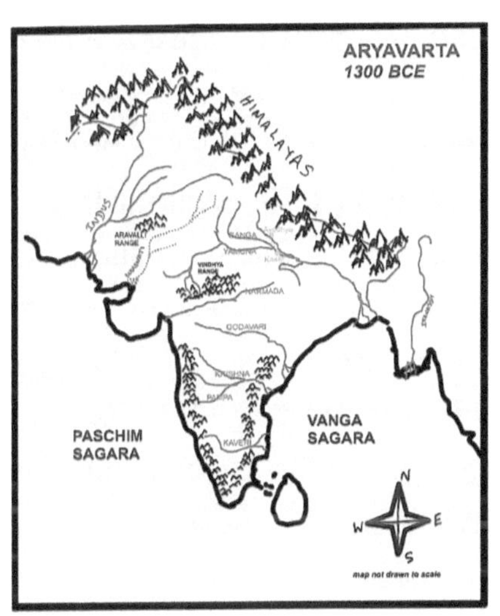

of Dharma. Rama is a popular ruler. In his rule, trade by land and sea is once again flourishing with lands afar—from the Kemet, the Land of Pyramids in the West to Ch'in, the land of silk in the East to the Dravida Desa and Lanka in the South. Political stability prevails within the kingdom. The ancient feud between the warring clans of Suryavanshis and Chandravanshis has been contained.

But has Rama ruled for too long? The vast Kosala Empire is fragile. Beneath this seemingly tranquil era, underlying tensions persist, with historical animosities between the Bharatas and Purus still smoldering. New competition from the Nagvanshis has emerged. Ayodhya's allies are still not strong enough to face another enemy as powerful as them. Although Ravana and his ten commanders were vanquished in Lanka, there were still remnants of his kin that had escaped, and their whereabouts remained shrouded in mystery. Have they regrouped?

Rama is staring at these challenges just at a time when he was contemplating the future of his Raghu-vamsa lineage. He is mindful of the need to prevent internal strife among his progenies. The enduring legacy of his clan is replete with stories of how his ancestors have sacrificed power and positions just to uphold Dharma. At the same time, Rama's scions, although united, are starting to become restless. What should Rama do? Rama weighs his options. He contemplates splitting the kingdom among his scions, mindfully aware of the balance he must strike between fairness, equity, and stability. For, in the crucible of decision, Rama's choices shall not merely shape the contours of his realm, but also the very destiny of generations yet unborn.

Rama seeks the counsel of his advisers, consisting of his brothers, Hanuman, and Jambavan along with Guru Vasishta and Rishi Rishyasringa. This Inner Council underscores the importance of protecting the kingdom by fortifying its borders to protect it from internal and external threats. Rama formulates his vision of creating a nation that is able to protect its borders, a country with a strong and sustainable economy, a civilization that espouses social justice, and a place that attracts the brightest of scholars from all over the world.

Lakshmana, Bharata, and Shatrugna set forth to assist their sons in governing the lands that Rama had identified. Lakshmana guides his sons through storytelling, reminiscing key events from the adventures he shared with Rama over their long years together. Meanwhile, a personal calamity arises. A secretive cult led by Yama tries to use their sorcery to manipulate and sway Rama to their way of life. The arrival of a reputed scholar in Ayodhya sets forth a series of events that ultimately results in Lakshmana's banishment from the kingdom. All this puts Rama in great mental turmoil. Can he overcome his personal afflictions to focus on matters concerning the present and future of his kingdom? Can he still live up to his reputation as a leader with vision, capable of motivating his people, and as one who adheres to Dharma?

Author's Note

They say there are over three hundred versions, over a thousand retellings, and countless variations of the great epic—Adi-Kavya—Ramayana, originally composed by Valmiki. This timeless epic has been retold and reinterpreted countless times since its compilation in the 7th century BCE. Until then, the epic was orally transmitted, leading to diverse versions emerging across cultures. While Valmiki's rendition serves as a foundational text, subsequent retellings have added new chapters and perspectives, enriching its narrative. Each version offers unique insights into themes of duty, honor, and righteousness, resonating with audiences worldwide. One thing that has remained true is the fact that the Ramayana continues to endure as a source of inspiration and introspection, transcending time and boundaries.

Like most Indian kids of my generation, the first time I heard the story of Ramayana was from my maternal grandfather Shri SR Ramanujam. SRR thatha, as we called him, was known for his linguistic skills as he was fluent in English, Sanskrit, and Tamil. What he was not known for were the skills of interacting with children. Yet, he always took time to tell me short stories. And every time he told me stories from Indian mythology, especially the Ramayana, it was never in one sitting nor was it a narration from start to finish. Rather, his style was always telling a story according to some context. He would suddenly tell one story, one episode, one chapter based on some incident that might have happened or based on his mood. Much later I learned to appreciate the beauty of such a nonlinear narrative style.

Like most people from my generation, I have seen movies and the first TV serial of Ramayan. I have also read English versions or translations written by Rajagopalachari (aka Rajaji) and Bibek Debroy. I have listened to the beautiful songs and bhajans on Ramayana composed by the Vaishnavite Alwar saints, poet Kambar, composer Tyagaraja, and bhakti movement icons such as Tulsidas and Jayadeva.

I am no scholar of the Ramayana nor is my reading list exhaustive. But anytime I read a version of this masterpiece, I get inspired in different ways. And each time I envision myself living in those times and living with the characters. I am what you would call someone that has 'rasana' in Sanskrit or 'rasanai' in Tamil. Unfortunately, there is no equivalent English word for this.

I consider myself a student first. A student of history and mythology. I have participated in countless debates that are a favorite pastime of Indians from my generation—i.e., did Ramayana and Mahabharata events take place in reality? Did all those characters in our mythologies and epics exist? And I found out that, surprisingly, it is not just among Indians. For I had presented a topic on the "Relevance of Ramayana in today's era," to American children from a middle school in Pennsylvania, USA. I learned that those kids were fascinated by this book and wanted to know more about Rama. And like most children, their favorite character was Hanuman. As it happened, their class teacher's husband, an American colleague from work, asked me if I could conduct an online session with the kids. I gladly accepted, of course. That was my first foray into articulating my views about Ramayana— replete with pictures, images, news clippings and whatnot!

As an ardent student of history, I am biased toward separating myths from facts. Like many people, I too believe that we Indians rarely took care in documenting or recording history in the form of buildings, carvings, or straight-jacketed literature. As frustrating as that can be, especially in comparison to Western or even Chinese historical records, Indian history is clothed in a derivative continuity of narrations across generations

My attempt through this book is in a way a continuation of that tradition. Similar in some respects, but different in most ways. This book is a compilation of 'my memories,' or "smarana," of certain portions of the Ramayana. And these memories are a record of the journey, or "yana" of Rama. In those records, I wished to capture the experiences of Rama, Lakshmana, and Sita. From such experiences, we can extract immortal and invaluable lessons on leadership.

At the crux of when I was to commence writing, I asked myself what would Rama and Lakshmana have 'felt?' How did Sita 'think?' How did Rama take decisions? Who did he consult? How did he execute his actions, improvising along the way with what is humanly possible? I also asked myself why Valmiki or other great authors did not elaborate on some of the moral dilemmas that Rama would have faced. In that, I have strived to stay away from the realm of mythology and fantasy or pure religious bhakti aspects. Because, to me, those approaches do not capture the story, nor do they capture the 'mind journey.' Equally important, I have strived to take the reader through the land, its history, and its people as I imagined it to be in those times.

In order to do justice to that perspective, I needed someone who knew, lived, and grew with Rama the most. That could only be Lakshmana. Thus, the narration in this book is done through his eyes or more specifically, his memories. Who better than Rama's own alter-ego, his shadow, his 'anuja,' to share with us those experiences?

For the story to be as realistic as possible, I have set the era to the period between the end of the Bronze Age and the onset of the Iron Age. It is my assumption that the events described in the story occurred somewhere around 1300 BCE, i.e., almost 3300 years ago. This is neither an authoritative fact nor a prejudiced opinion. It is my estimation and only that. I justify my assumptions using information on names from the Raghu-vamsa, stories from the Rig Veda, characters in Valmiki Ramayana, and Padma Purana, etc. Additional research about Iron Age weapons, geography, Bronze Age kingdoms, and human migration theories—specifically from the study of R1b haplogroup genomic studies and the connection of Sintashta people with the Indo-Aryan group are referenced from various published books, university theses, and articles.

All the stories are loosely based on translated versions of Valmiki Ramayana, Kambar's Rama-Avataram, and Padma Purana. However, to enhance the narration, I have added reimagined plots. For the names of characters, kingdoms, and geographies, I have tried to reference them also from Valmiki Ramayana. To embellish the story, I have introduced very few fictional characters. I sincerely apologize if that offends anyone or any community, as that is not my intent at all.

My 'Part' and 'Chapter' titles are inspired by the names of songs, or kritis, composed by the foremost devotional saint Thyagaraja of the 18th century CE. The musical touch is also a homage to the musical elegance of Valmiki Ramayana set to tune in the anustubh metre. It is said that Rama himself was captivated by this song when he heard it sung by his sons Luv and Kush in his court!

Thus, the starting words of kriti *'Saketa Nagara'* mean literally 'Ayodhya City;' *'Dharmaatma'* means literally 'Soul of Dharma;' *'Sitamma Mayamma'* means 'Sita is my mother;' *'Entaro maha anubhava'* means 'Many people have attained knowledge/ wisdom;' *'Chintis tu unnade yamudu'* means 'The God of death is filled with anxiety.' Hopefully, you, the reader, will find the connection of the title with the respective story.

Finally, I wish to mention my motivation to write this book. On an impulse to write a fictional plot on Ramayana or Mahabharata, I started a blog on fiction nearly 15 years ago. The link to that is mentioned below. However, the drive to really bring out leadership lessons based on Ramayana fructified early this year in a conversation with two of my close friends. When I mentioned that to my wife, she took it upon herself to motivate me and encourage me to write. At every step of the way, literally. During our evening walks, I have had the pleasure of bouncing my idea-of-the-day with her and often received excellent suggestions. I have also heavily relied upon my dear sister Priya to validate the story concepts, assumptions, and the style of writing. Equally inspiring have been conversations with my father, Shri Thambu, as well as with my lovely daughter. Their perspectives—coming from different generations—helped me adjust the flow of these stories. I have also relied upon a close group of friends to critique and provide feedback, and they have readily provided valuable tips that I have incorporated. Thus, it is to all these friends and family members to whom I am deeply indebted, without whose support this effort would have rusted in the corners of my mind.

To you, my dear reader, it is my intent and desire to give something for everyone. Perhaps one may wish to enjoy the imagination. Others may desire morals and lessons. Few others might opt for the historical and literary facts. And maybe it may bring out your own 'smarana' or memories from your childhood. Be that as it may, I fully acknowledge the multitude of choices you have in this genre of books. Thus, I thank you from the bottom of my heart for purchasing this book and supporting me.

Above everything else, I have an unwavering faith and devotion toward Lord Rama. For it is he who has guided me in conjuring the imaginative elements within this book. It is he who is the source of strength I needed to juggle both work and writing.

Characters

Term	Explanation
Agastya	Legendary sage and a great scholar and author of several puranic and Vedic texts
Ahalya	Sage Ahalya was a very reputed Rishi, the wife of sage Gautama and appears in several puranas. The most famous is her meeting of Rama in Valmiki Ramayana
Angada	Son of Vali, prince of Kishkinda
Bhagiratha	Ancestor of Rama
Bujanga and Dattagama	Fictional names of elders in the court of Kishkinda

Term	Explanation
Chandraketu and Chitrangada	Sons of Laksmana
Dasharatha	Father of Rama and emperor of Ayodhya, coming from a long line of Raghu-vamsa
Dumma	A fictional character, portrayed as Sage Vasishta's disciple
Durvasa Atriputra	Sage Durvasa was a famous rishi and scholar, authoring several slokas in Vedas. He belongs to the Turvasu clan. His name appears in several puranas and itihasa, including Ramayanaand Mahabharat
Garuda	Mythological Eagle-bird like god, vehicle of Lord Vishnu
Gautama	Sage Ahalya was a very reputed Rishi, the husband of sage Ahalya and appears in several puranic stories
Harishchandra	Ancestor of Rama

Term	Explanation
Ikshvaku	Legendary ancestor of Rama and a progeny of the original Bharata
Indra, Mitra and Varuna	Vedic gods that were worshipped not just in Bharat, but also in Iran and Syria. Indo-Aryan deities Mitra, Varuna, Indra, and Nasatya (Ashvins) are listed and invoked in two treaties found in Hattusa, between the kings Sattiwaza of Mitanni and Šuppiluliuma I the Hittite in 1330 BCE
Jambavan	Warrior and senior advisor to Rama
Janaka	Father of Sita
Janakamma	Fictional character
Jatayu	The legendary vulture king that tries to rescue Sita from Ravana, when he was abducting her, but fails in that ensuing fight

Term	Explanation
Kaikeyi	Third wife of Dasharatha and mother of Bharata, from the kingdom of Kekeya
Kakutstha	Another ancestor of Rama. In Valmiki Ramayan, Vishwamitra addresses Rama as 'Kakutsha Rama'
Kama	In Hindy mythology, he is the God of Love; In this story, he is portrayed as someone that was defeated by Lord Rudra
Kausalya	First wife of Dasharatha and mother of Rama
Kubera	In the Hindu mythology, he is the half-brother of Ravana and is also known as Visravana. In this book, he is portrayed as a leader of the Nagvanshis naval fleet
Kumbakarna	Younger brother of Ravana. Stood by Ravana's side throughout

Term	Explanation
Manu	Considered as the original King that codified Vedic laws. Possibly an early Aryan king, although some scholars believe he was a Pandya King
Mareecha	Son of Tataka, and uncle of Ravana. Mentioned in both 'Bala Kandam' as well as in 'Sundara Kandam'
Meghananda	Son of Ravana. Also called as Indrajit
Muruga	A very popular and prominent Dravidian God, believed as the Tamil name for Lord Karthikeya or Lord Subrahmanya or Lord Skanda, who is mentioned as the son of Shiva and Parvati, in Hindu mythology. Rig Veda (hymn 5.2), Valmiki Ramayana has references to Lord Skanda. 1st CE coins depict him as 'Kumara'
Nagamma	Fictional character

Term	Explanation
Nala and Nila	Twins of the Vanar clan, that played a significant part in the construction of Ram Setu
Narada	A legendary and mythological sage and scholar. Appears in several Vedic and Upanishadic texts. He is considered to have told Valmiki about Rama and encourages Valmiki to write a book on Rama's life
Parasurama	Sixth avatar of Vishnu. Considered to be the founder of Chera country. Appears briefly in Ramayana to challenge Rama to lift his bow of Vishnu, which Rama easily does
Raghu	Ancestor of Rama
Rishabha	Ancestor of Rama. Also considered as the first Tirthankara in the Jain texts
Rishyashringa	Rishi Rishyashringa was a very famous and learned scholar, authoring several shlokas in the Vedas.

Term	Explanation
Rudra	Mentioned in Rig Vedic texts a great Lord. Opinion is divided if this represented Shiva himself from pre-Vedic times
Sagara	Ancestor of Rama
Sampaati	Brother of Jataayu
Sara	Fictional character
Sesha	Another name for Lakshmana
Shanta	Mentioned in some puranic texts as the elder sister of Rama. She was the first child and daughter of Dasharatha, who gave her to be adopted by the King of Kalinga, who was a close ally of Dasharatha. She was married to Rishi Rishyashringa
Shiva	pre-Rig Vedic god. Worshipped as one of the trinity of gods in the later-day Vedic tradition
Subahu	Another son of Tataka, but dies at the hands of Rama

Term	Explanation
Sudas Paijavana	Legendary king of the Bharatas clan that ruled in approximately the modern Sutlej river area. Son (or Grandson) of Divodas. Finds mention in Rig Veda as the King that fought and defeated ten kings, led by the Purus clan. He had both Vishwamitra as well as Vasishta as his advisor/head priest. Some scholars believe he commissioned the composition of Rig Veda
Sugreeva	King of Kishkinda and younger brother of Vali
Sumitra	Second wife of Dasharatha and mother of twins Lakshmana & Shatrugna
Surpanakha	Sister of Ravana and someone with sharp (surpha) talon like nails (nakha). Mentioned in Valmiki Ramayanaas the person responsible for coveting Rama, but in the process gets her nose and ears chopped by Lakshmana.

Term	Explanation
	She then complains to Ravana that sets in motion a series of events that ends in Lanka battle. Her entry into the epic is thought by some scholars as one of the most important turning points of the Ramayana
Suvahu and Surasena	Sons of Shatrugna
Taksha and Pushkar	Sons of Bharata
Tataka	Leader of Yaksha's who traditionally had a dispute with established order as prescribed by Vedic Brahmins
Urmila	Wife of Lakshmana, and sister of Sita
Vali	King of Kishkinda and elder brother of Sugreeva

Term	Explanation
Valmiki	The author of first Ramayana. Contemporary of Rama. His ashram (or residential school) is where Sita delivered Luv and Kush and spent her last days, as she was banished from Kosala.
Vasishta	Guru of the Ikshvaku dynasty. Some scholars view the name as a title rather than one individual. Thus, 'Vashista' appears in Rig Veda as well as in epics such as Ramayana, although these were supposedly authored several centuries apart
Vedavati	Another name for Sita
Vibhishana	Brother of Ravana, and succeeds him as the rule of Lanka
Visravana	Half-brother of Ravana. Some scholars believe it is another name for Kubera (or Kuvera)

Term	Explanation
Yama	In the Hindu puranas, he is the God of Death. In this book, he is portrayed as a clan leader of Nagvanshis.

Contents

Part 1 – Sum of parts greater than the whole

|| Saketa Nagara ||

Chapter 1

Rama's Summer Retreat

Ayodhya, 1300 BCE

Rama was on the grounds of his summer retreat, standing on the lawns near the edge of the woods. It was a typical summer evening, with the sun still high in the sky and the atmosphere hot and dry. He was practicing archery by shooting arrows at different targets. Adjacent to him were several weapons laid out neatly on a table. As I approached them, I saw Bharata watching Rama practice from one side. There was another tall muscular man on the other side watching Rama. Ah, Hanuman! I hadn't seen him for over a year now. Not surprising, as he never stays in one place and is always traveling. His role as the 'Spy Chief' of our kingdom Kosala requires him to be everywhere, and nowhere in particular. In other words, go where there is action but don't let yourself be seen. And Hanuman fits that profile to a tee. Oh, and those mischievous, sparkling eyes, always coming up with the next prank. But strangely, besides these three gents, no one else was here. Neither the attendants nor the guards were to be seen. Well, I admit I was quite surprised when I got a missive from Rama a few days back, asking me and my brothers to join him at his summer retreat. Shatrugna and I set out immediately. Bharata came separately but must have reached ahead of us.

As I came near, Rama said, without taking his eyes off his target, "Lakshmana, watch the arrowhead closely as I release the arrow. It will first rotate on its axis and then eventually stabilize, but it will appear as if it is traveling in a steady direction." Sure enough, the arrow found its mark one *paridesh*[1] away. I wasn't surprised that it hit the target. After all it was Rama that was shooting it. But there was something curious about the arrow's trajectory. He aimed it much flatter than normal, yet it hit the mark. The bowstring was a double helix instead of a single strand. And, as Rama said, the arrow did appear to be spiraling toward the target. Overall, the arrow appeared heavier and shinier than the normal ones. And then I noticed that there was a metal end cap with two feathers at the end. We don't make ours that way. We just have a groove cut on

---

1   *paridesh* – an ancient unit of measurement of distances; 1 *paridesh* = 125 feet

Astra – Weapon

the far end of the shaft, which we need to place on the single stranded bowstring. All in all, I was intrigued about this improvised weapon.

"It is not perfect, but it will do. I am even thinking of calling this *Brahma-astra*, or the *'weapon of Lord Brahma himself*,'" Rama chuckled, as he continued to practice.

"Hello to you too, brother!" I cooed and added, "Have you called us all the way here for a naming ceremony for some weapons?" Shatrugna laughed aloud, but I got a nudge in my stomach from Bharata. I shared an easy camaraderie with Rama, but Bharata usually maintained a bit more formal relationship. Rama placed his bow back on the table, came over, and hugged us. Hanuman too came over and we all embraced each other.

After the initial greetings and enquiries were over, we went to sit by the nearby stream under a shade. The flow of water, although thin, gave a slight reprieve from the intense heat that this region had been having all summer. We all sat there quietly for some time. The air was hot and heavy, and not necessarily from the heat. I sensed something else was going on, for Rama to have called us all here, alone.

Finally, Rama broke the silence and said, "Brothers, I have been thinking. It has been nearly twenty years since I was crowned King of *Kosala*. During this time, our kingdom has expanded, our *Aryavarta* nation is relatively peaceful, and the rule of our *Dharma*[2] prevails. I cannot imagine having ruled all this without your uncompromising loyalty and commitment in pursuit of protecting our kingdom. Yet, these two decades are starting to take a toll on me. My mind is not at peace. I wish to plan for the future of *Ayodhya*."

There! He said it. So, this was what has been on his mind. In his typical style, Rama comes to the point with a simple, yet straightforward line. It is not a surprise that our father used to call him a "man of one word!" Well, now that I think about what Rama said, there has been a flurry of activities of late back at our royal court. Messengers, important citizens of Ayodhya, trade merchants, foreign emissaries from various kingdoms, craftsmen of metallurgy, artists, and artisans, were all seen coming and seeking an audience with Rama.

While some of this is not uncommon, the frequency of these meetings was unusual. Most of these visitors sought private audiences with Rama. I normally get to know the details, but I admit that even I was not kept informed of most of these visits.

---

2   ***Dharma*** – While no exact English equivalent exists for this word, it approximately signifies 'code of conduct'

Hanuman too had been away from the capital for over a year—I am meeting him only today—so I haven't yet been able to connect all those visits to what Rama just said. Shatrugna spoke first: "Ram *bhayya*[3], why are you speaking like this? Yes, it has been two decades, but you are well and capable of ruling for a lifetime. You have earned every right to have done so. As you said, when everything is going well, why change anything? Did someone say something?"

When Shatrugna asked if someone said something, he was, of course, alluding to that painful episode almost twenty years ago when some rumors circulating at that time caused Rama and Sita *bhabhi* to get separated. At that time, we were all shocked by his decision to leave her in Sage Valmiki's ashram outside our kingdom. Rama had just been crowned King of Kosala, and soon after this episode occurred. He did not want to start his rule with a blot on our family name. But that was then. Rama's rule has since ushered in a golden age in all Aryavarta, to a point where people universally loved him, and Rama left no scope for any rumors. So, after all these years, we weren't expecting Rama to have such a conversation with us. Thus, Shatrugna was naturally right in alluding to possible rumors fueling Rama's thoughts.

---

3   *bhayya* – brother;
     bhabhi – sister-in-law;

Anyway, Rama didn't react to that. Shatrugna further added: "Ram bhayya, rumors or not, it doesn't matter. The people are all happy and some are even calling this period 'Ram Rajya[4].' We are honored to have been born as your brothers. It is our duty to serve you and our people well." Rama shot a glance at me. I just shrugged my shoulders and said, "Just take me wherever you go after you retire."

I might have said that in a lighter tone, but I meant every word of it. I have been around Rama throughout my life, and I have no desire to change that. Besides, our sons have all just recently got married and have gone to their respective in-laws' places with their respective brides. Our city Ayodhya still wore a festive look after weeks of endless functions, rituals and parties. But then, Rama's timing is always impeccable. If he has thought about something, two things are true. One, he has thought it through fully from all possible angles, and two, he has set his mind to achieve that.

Rama looked at us all and said, "I know the amount of love and respect you have for me. But hear me out. As much as I feel fine health-wise, there are some practical matters that require my undivided attention. You might have noticed that the past few weeks have been quite hectic. I have been meeting people from

---

4   ***Rajya*** *– literally rule;* ***Ram Rajya*** *– rule of Rama. However, it is associated with a glorious, prosperous rule, in general.*

across various spectrums, from royalty to craftsmen. To top it all, we have successfully conducted the marriage ceremonies for our children. Their marriage alliances with respectable royal families should further cement the relationship with our allies. Shatrugna, I realize that there are several things that are going well for us. It is precisely why the timing is right for me to think about my successor. I spoke to Bharata earlier about becoming the next ruler of this throne. After all, he has the experience of ruling this kingdom before, but he has rejected my proposal. He has expressed his desire to go to his maternal place in Kekeya and eventually retire.

Therefore, I would be truly happy if you both take my place here. The sons of Queen Mother Sumitra deserve to rule this place as much as any of us."

Shatrugna and I looked at each other, shocked. Neither of us had any inkling about this. More importantly, neither of us have ever desired the throne. Our mother Sumitra and later our respective wives have always maintained that we should not aspire for separate territories. Thus, I wanted to object to Rama's proposal, but for some reason, I was tongue-tied as I was caught unawares. Thankfully, my twin Shatrugna intervened. He and I usually can complete each other's sentences. Our thoughts are one and our actions similar. So, I am not surprised that he was able to articulate my exact thoughts and said: "Brother, how could you even think of such a situation where we must live a life separated from you, again? Have Lakshmana and I ever given you that indication of our desire to rule an independent kingdom? Besides, we are all the same age. At this stage in our life, we too wish to retire along with you, whenever you decide that course of action. More importantly, we have raised our sons to always be on the side of their cousins and to never desire the throne. Thus, there won't be any cause for concern if and when you declare Luv and Kush as your heirs."

Rama became a bit emotional at this display of loyalty and passion. He embraced Shatrugna and said: "Forgive me, my dearest Shatrugna. In the state of mind that I find myself of late, if I have hurt your feelings, my apologies."

Over the next few moments, we clarified each other's wishes and made it clear that none of us desired any part of the kingdom. Finally, we all agreed to take the advice of our Guru before arriving at a decision.

The sun was setting, and we decided to get inside the King's house. I deliberately said 'house' and not a 'palace,' because this summer retreat was housed amidst a lush garden surrounded by exotic trees, with deer, peacocks, and rabbits freely roaming and a small stream flowing on one side of the lawn, which is where we were having our conversation earlier. But the building itself was a simple one-story house where at most two individuals can stay. The furnishings were simple, basic and just about enough for an average person. Hardly fit for a King with the stature and age of Rama. Yet, it was here that Rama went to spend some time once in a while. As this is his private retreat, I do not exactly know what he does there. But I have heard from the security staff that at times he could be spending several days at a stretch alone, holed inside the house with even the attendants not allowed to bring food or water. Rama has more than earned his right to have his space and privacy away from the busy life of Ayodhya. Till now, none of us have been inside his quarters, so we were all curious to see what we would find inside. When we entered, the first thing, rather the only thing, we all saw was a life-size golden statue. All of us, except Rama, just stood back at the door as if in a trance. The first person to make a move was Hanuman, who ran and prostrated before the statue and sobbed. Indeed, I fought to hold back my tears, but we all went near and bowed before it. The statue was that of **Sita!**

Chapter 2

Hanuman Reveals the Secret of Nagvanshis

Sita bhabhi had passed away almost a decade back. But it had been even longer since she moved out of Ayodhya. Rama had steadfastly refused to remarry, despite alliance requests and entreaties from various kingdoms. I had heard that Rama had commissioned the crafting of a golden statue of Sita bhabhi and thought about placing it on the throne in her absence. However, this is the first time I am seeing it. I could not believe my eyes. A life-size statue of bhabhi. The resemblance, the striking pose, the proud upright chin unique to the womenfolk of her clan, the *Jahnus*, all brought back fond memories of my great bhabhi.

It was late afternoon. We freshened up a bit and went outside to the porch. The attendants by now had prepared dinner and made a small fire. The five of us sat beside the fire and were served our meals. Afterwards, the attendants cleaned the place and left us by ourselves.

Bharata opened the conversation: "Bhayya, earlier you were practicing with some weapons. I noticed that they were a bit different from the typical ones we use. Where did you get them and why were you practicing, or shall I say, 'testing' them?" Rama placed his hands closer to the fire flames, then rubbed his palms and smiled at Bharata. The twinkle in his eyes told me that he had something interesting to share with us and was perhaps waiting for someone to bring up that topic. "Ah! I was wondering when one of you clever gents would ask me about that. But perhaps it is best that Hanuman speaks about those, as he was the one who brought them here yesterday," said Rama.

Hanuman shriveled up a bit. He usually does when everyone turns their attention to him. He clearly didn't enjoy any spotlight. He first looked at Rama, as if seeking his acquiescence to speak, then at us, and then finally spoke: "My Lords. I came here yesterday, after having spent over a year traveling to quite a few parts of our great nation. About a year back, I was visiting the city of *Masanga* near my birthplace in *Kishkinda*. There, I chanced upon some traders that were dealing with weapons that did not look anything like the ones that we are used to. I was curious about these weapons but could not place where they sourced them from. When I tested some of the weapons, I realized they were superior in quality and exotic in design. I asked the traders to take me to their source, but they refused. This naturally spurred me to investigate this matter further. Over the next several days, I went in disguise with an assumed name of *Marut*—a rich merchant from the land of *mlecchas*[5]. I was looking to track down these traders' money trail, which I felt was the easiest way to track the source of these weapons. My path took me from one place to another.

Eventually, I, as Marut, received an invitation from the wealthy Chyavana merchant guild. So I visited them in their capital city, Maihar. This place is about five days from here in Ayodhya by boat. As a community, the Chyavanas keep to themselves and are rarely seen mingling with outsiders. Their legend places them as descendants of Lord Parashuram, who, as we all know, headed the Haihayas clan with their capital city Mahismati, on the banks of River Narmada. Lord Parashuram subsequently also established an independent kingdom in the South Western part of Dravida Nadu. He named it the Cheralam, established a just rule, and very prominently declared his followers as '*Nagvanshis.*' You may well be aware of the long-standing dispute between the major groupings of Aryavartans—us Suryavanshis and the Chandravanshis. And at times we have fought with each other as well. Although Lord Parashuram strove to remain equidistant

---

5   ***mlecchas*** *– Sanskrit term to address barbaric foreign tribes*

from both groups, he has occasionally clashed with one or the other clans. Besides him, the Nagvanshis have produced several excellent warriors, leaders, and scholars such as Guru *Vishwamitra*, Sage *Agastya*, and even Lanka King *Ravana*. Their chief deity is Lord Muruga, who goes by other names such as Karthikeya or Skanda or Kumara.

Anyway, in his final years, Lord Parashuram wished to retire in the Himalayas. Some of his followers accompanied him from Mahismati, a few stayed back, but others settled in Maihar. There, they intermingled with other local tribes of that region and established their new base. *Maihar* itself is situated at the top of the *Kaimur hills* that run between the *Sone River* and the *Ganga River* and offers a strategic view from atop in case of any incoming enemies. Not that these people have ever been in any major war of late, but they are generally of a distrusting disposition and are always battle-ready. That is evident from the martial arts training that all of them—man and woman alike— are required to undertake. I reckon they must have originally been trained by Lord *Parashuram* himself.

As an interested and wealthy merchant, I as Marut, had access to most of their places. So, I spent a few days there and learned that they had excellent trade contacts with most of the Dravida Kingdoms— likely owing to their shared culture. Although closer to us by distance, they, how shall I say it, 'maintain their distance' from us!"

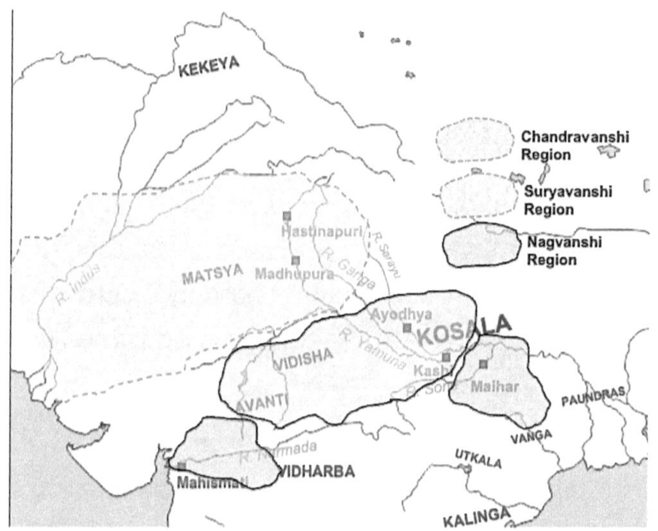

Hanuman took a pause to catch his breath. Thank the good Lord! A topic of this nature post dinner, albeit interesting, was making my eyes droop a bit. I have also had a long day riding in the heat to reach this place.

Hanuman glanced at each one of us, and sensing that there were no questions, he continued, "Besides trade networks, the Chyavanas are very good metallurgists. They seem to have perfected some new techniques to forge '*ayas*[6],' i.e., alloy metals, of six different kinds. Specifically, the *śyāma-Ayas* and

6   *Ayas* – ore; *śyāma* – dark, and refers to Iron; **Lohita** – shining, refers to Copper or Bronze

Lohita-Ayas seem to produce much better weapons. Neither of these metals are unfamiliar to us, but as you may know, we traditionally use them to make tools only for agriculture, construction, and cooking."

Bharata intervened here, a little ticked off, and asked: "Hanuman, are you saying you procured some weapons from these people? If so, you should have brought it to my attention first before disturbing Ram bhayya at his private retreat. As head of security, I am responsible for procuring weapons, and you know that."

Hanuman looked a little flabbergasted at this sharp rebuttal by Bharata. Rama intervened and said: "Bharata, don't admonish Hanuman. I had asked him to come here with a sample of those weapons. In any case, these were not procured, rather they were gifted to this rich merchant Marut! Pray, let him proceed with completing his story, although be prepared for learning some mundane aspects of our land." That mollified Bharata. And it sure dusted off the tiredness out of me. Seemed like there was more to this besides being a bedtime story!

The ever-polite Hanuman continued: "Thank you, Lord Ram and Lord Bharat. Yes, these weapons are all gifts from a few other places that I went to. And not just from Maihar. As you can guess, the real reason for their invitation to me was that they had been redesigning weapons with new-age methods of smelting, and they wanted to find a large-scale weapons buyer like me. Thankfully, my cover identity checked out as I had established an elaborate ruse. As you very well know, the weapons manufacturing technology itself is not new to us. Our ancestors have been doing this for over five hundred years. However, we have mostly made it by smelting metals having low melting points. That made the products unfit for very high-intensity uses. Only a few people are aware of the fact that the Ahar-Banas tribe, out in the Western part of Malwa area by the ancient River Saraswati, were one of the first people to extract this metal. Subsequently, their know-how had spread to a few parts of our nation, as well as other parts of the world. Yet not everyone can do this as well as they do, as this ore hasn't been found in many places. Thus, due to lack of support from kings or due to limited availability of people with the know-how, this knowledge has remained concentrated in very few parts of our nation."

Ah! My favorite subject. I love weapons and pride myself in knowing everything about weapons – their usage, their manufacturing, and just about anything. And by now I was fully awake and tuned to the topic. I intervened, to show off my knowledge: "Extracting is one thing, Hanuman. Traditionally, the ayas would be forged from mold-casting techniques to produce knives or spears, but the edges often get chipped. And as far as I know, most armies still face that challenge. Are you saying someone was able to overcome that limitation and have produced products for very high-intensity uses such as weapons or heavy construction equipment?" If he was irritated by my trivial question, Hanuman is not the one to show his true reactions.

He continued explaining patiently: "You are correct, Lord Lakshman. A new technique is what these Chyavanas have hit upon. They have been able to forge thin strips of this śyāma-ayas, which they then beat together and fuse to get billets. They then shape these billets to make many products. The high carbon content in the śyāma-ayas makes it possible for them to produce such thin strips. Of course, these people are blessed with a region that is rich in such grades of ore, and they have an end-to-end ecosystem of extraction, processing, and manufacturing-related know-how. Above all, their cultural identity of retaining a martial arts way of life allows them to innovate with newer weapons. From what I could gather, they have created or modified weapons such as double-edged daggers, ax sockets, axes with broad cutting edges, arrowheads with socketed tangs, spearheads, sickles, crowbars, lances, and spades."

Bharata was a bit worried and in a thoughtful tone asked: "Okay fine, they seem to have cracked the code. But you mentioned earlier that the Nagvanshis are very independent people and don't try to intervene in broader Aryavarta politics. Has the mastery over weapons given them new ammunition, so to speak?"

Hanuman replied: "Not exactly, Lord Bharat. The Chyavanas have recently started selling their wares with a few of their traditional trading partners. These are mostly merchant guilds and middlemen from places far South from here, such as *Korkai* in *Tamil desa* and *Pazhayannur* in the land of *Cheralam*. I found out about these places only by following the trail of their weapons trade. And sure enough, there seems to be a rising interest from those kingdoms. My sources tell me that the Chyavanas' trading network stretches from *Shortugai*, a city that lies to the northwest of *Kekeya*, all the way to the South in *Lanka*! Presently, they are not able to produce these new-age weapons on a large-scale but are quite close to doing so. Imagine if they start doing so. Soon our enemies will have much better weapons than us. Or worse, the Nagvanshis might openly start rebelling against our suzerainty over their domain. As much as they are on relatively friendly terms with us, a monopoly on cutting-edge technology can always be tempting for anyone to start acting superior. I laid out these details and my views in a report that I sent a month back to Lord Rama. He directed me to get a few samples and meet him here as soon as possible."

When Hanuman finished narrating all this, there was just a silent admiration for his tenacity to go after facts, mastery of details, and ability to present a comprehensive picture of the problem at hand. That Hanuman had these traits even in his younger days was something that only Rama was able to spot. When Rama became the King of Kosala two decades back, he had immediately appointed Hanuman to set up a *spash*, or spy network. Bharata profusely apologized for his earlier outburst and commended Hanuman for his foresight and smart thinking.

I responded by saying: "Hanuman, you are simply brilliant. You have neither lost your talent to get into any disguise nor your ability to go undercover, even after all these years. Yet, something about this doesn't add up in my mind. You say that the Chyavanas are invoking their roots and trying to peddle their wares to other Nagvanshis. However, I don't think this is possible without leadership and planning. After years of maintaining peace with us, why a sudden change in their strategy? Do you know who their leader is? Is he somehow orchestrating it? In your assumed role as a rich merchant, surely this person would have tried to meet with you, yes?"

Hanuman replied: "Thank you, Lord Lakshman. You are again absolutely correct in this assumption. This suspicion was playing in my mind constantly. But this was the most vexing part of my investigation. Try as I might, I was never able to get anyone to talk about their source of funding or reveal the identity of their leader. Any amount of bribe I offered could still not fetch this answer. It appeared as if each trader or middleman was just that. The Chyavanas had compartmentalized information such that each one only dealt with someone one level above them. They are trained not to ask questions. In the spy world, we call it 'deniability.' Even if one arm is cut, the head remains. This sort of a structure is not easy to implement in a kingdom such as ours, due to our diverse structure. Whereas it is much easier to do so in a smaller, homogenous entity such as that of the Nagvanshis. That said, if given more time I should be able to crack that missing puzzle. However, I had to rush back here on Lord Ram's orders."

Rama then said: "You see my brothers? There is danger lurking. We seem to have a potential threat near our home. Based on all the things we know, I don't think it is an easy task to simply confront the Chyavanas. They will of course deny everything and we don't have a shred of proof. Instead, I think we should find a way to lure them with bait. We have to be the first buyer of their technology. We should not just buy their products, but we should recruit their experts. If we lay hands on their know-how, we can control their source of income. That, in my mind, would diminish their strength.

Now, coming back to the arrowhead you saw earlier, it was made of this śyāma-ayas that has a black polish finish. Not only that, but during the forging process, they seem to have shaped the surface conically. To keep the symmetry, they have etched faces in four directions around this conical surface. I think the name '*Brahma-astra*' suits it, as it reminds me of the four faces of Lord Brahma. But speaking from a structural aspect, this metal-alloy, or śyāma-ayas, is also heavier than the ones we use. Hence, these people have smartly come up with a cap at the other end of the arrow shaft that acts like a counterweight to provide balance. The feathers attached to the end cap are not just for aesthetic look. Rather, it provides just the right lift when it is released from the bow, even when there is heavy wind. Similarly, there are other innovations done on existing weapons. But Hanuman tells me that this is just the start. They are starting to build factories and workshops to experiment with new innovations. While Hanuman was not allowed entry to any of those, he thinks he can penetrate those workshops."

Shatrugna, who was keenly listening to all this, spoke in a measured tone: "Ram bhayya. If what you say is all true, then surely, we shouldn't be seen resting on our past laurels. That said, I still don't understand why you must think about succession? Isn't this new information a just cause for your continued leadership? If you agree, please give your orders. We shall set forth to various parts of our nation and gather even more intelligence, know-how or if possible, bring those experts back here to set up workshops and factories."

Rama looked at him with a mix of affection and admiration for a few minutes, and said, "Well-spoken Shatrugna. That is what we will do. However, it shouldn't be you that has to go all over our land. As you said, now is the time for us to show leadership. And a hallmark of a good leader is one that provides a vision for his people, empowers them and supports them where necessary. So, let us display collective leadership and entrust our sons with this assignment. This is a perfect opportunity for them to take this challenge. We should draw up specific assignments for each of them. Our strategy must be to modernize our armory, adapt our training methods for our soldiers, deepen our spy-and-intelligence network and lastly expand our domain. Not just that, as Ayodhya must fund this project, we also need to find ways to modernize our treasury. I need each of you to oversee respective areas. We shall each mentor our sons in guiding them with their respective tasks.

Brothers, I now feel much more relaxed after discussing this with you. There is work ahead of us. And we need additional information. Hanuman, send word to your men that are covering these outer parts of Aryavarta and gather intelligence about śyāma-ayas ores. How do the local people extract them? Also draw a map showing each of their nearest trading posts. Bring back your findings and meet us in Ayodhya. Lakshmana, inform our sons to assemble back in Ayodhya and plan to convene our Inner Council. Bharata, send your men to keep a watch on the Chyavanas' external trade routes. We may pick up some more clues. Who knows who they are trading with outside of our land? Let us all plan to meet a month from now back at Ayodhya."

Chapter 3

Decision of the Inner Council

Almost a month has passed since our meeting at Rama's summer place. I woke up early this morning. We have a big day ahead and possibly a long one. This past month has been hectic, what with several information gathering sessions, meeting several messengers and planning for the arrival of my sons and nephews. The last task had to be planned and done in a clandestine manner. Rama did not want everyone to get wind of what we were about to discuss at the Council. Even our sons were given as little information as possible. There has been rapid progress in our preparation. We had to keep the circle of people that were in-the-know to a very small number. I parried several questions and offers of assistance from my own inner staff and ministers. All said, I was eagerly looking forward to the Council meeting this morning.

But before that, let me share some details about the functioning of the Council, the grand assembly, or the maha-sabha, and the building itself. The Assembly Hall was a semi-circular shaped building, facing East. All public buildings of the Suryavanshis, or the dynasty affiliated to the sun, always faced East. The front side of the hall has a large courtyard with a dome-shaped roof. There is then a walkway with fragrant flower plants lined up on either side, supported by shade-giving trees on the outer walkway. It was provisioned to allow visitors to get down from their chariots, horses, or palanquins and enter the hall directly. The Hall itself can host up to two hundred seats and has a seating area for five hundred people. Whenever the larger assembly was in session, we typically got representatives from all over Aryavarta and, at times, from foreign dignitaries, and often a special representative. The Inner Council consists of eight of us, including Rama, and decisions are made by voting on a motion that is put forth to the assembly. All members get equal voting rights. As per our Samhita, or law, the King is required to act on the advice of the Council but can veto their advice, should he deem it necessary. But I don't recall the last time Rama used these veto powers.

On this day, the members were starting to assemble. I saw Guru Vasishta and Jambavan seated next to each other. Hanuman and us brothers sat together. The last member was Sage Rishyasringa, who is a great scholar and also happened to be the husband of our late elder sister Shanta.

Looking at Sage Rishyasringa reminded me of our late sister Shanta. A great soul. The last I saw her was during mine and my brothers' wedding. Even when we were toddlers, our father allowed Shanta didi to be adopted by his good friend, the King of Vanga. Ever since, whenever we went on our vacations to Vanga desa to visit *didi*, we had a lovely time. Because our sister pampered us, told stories, and spoiled us with the inordinate variety of sweets that the land of Vanga was known for. Although a princess, she and Sage Rishyasringa lived in a beautiful hermitage by the banks of the gorgeous river Mahanadi. A welcome distraction from the hustle and bustle of Ayodhya. Shanta didi had attained the feet of the Lord a few years back, but it was good to see my brother-in-law, the wise, learned, and kind Rishyasringa. Now, back from memories of my past and on to the proceedings of the assembly!

As I was saying, today, the Inner Council was assembled with little or no pronouncements, and there weren't too many visitors or guests. As the Council members took their seats, a hushed silence fell. Rama purveyed the members with a rather somber expression. All the serving attendants and close entourage members were dismissed to maintain the secrecy of the conversation. Even after all these years, there was a strange premonition of a powerful invisible Nagvanshi foe that might have their eyes and ears trained on us. My brother Bharata, as per tradition, rose up to officially start the proceedings. He first paid respects to the wise sages, welcomed the members, and then turned to Rama to address the assembly.

Rama spoke: "Wise members of the Council. For over three decades, you have guided me in establishing a rule of Dharma. The elders of this august Assembly have ensured that our lineage – the *Raghu-vamsa* – did not swerve away from its responsibilities. I have been blessed and fortunate to have brothers like these who have stood by me and taken care of various aspects of administration. While the rest of the known world is going through wars and famine, your blessings have helped maintain peace, stability, and prosperity over the greater Bharata Desa.

However, our Kosala, although viewed as a protectorate by many smaller kingdoms within Aryavarta, is getting dormant. We are not innovating fast enough. We have not changed much over decades. Our sources tell me that there are places that have innovated on newer weapons technology, and there are places that have a revolutionary way of administering their society. We should be able to do these things too. We have to work harder to catch up with the times.

My wish is to structure our overall administration to enable such a transition.

Long years of stable and peaceful rule indeed have their advantages, but the downside is that our society is becoming complacent. Maintaining peace and stability for such a long time has taken a toll on me and my brothers. That brings me to my second wish.

My brothers and I do not intend to rule for much longer. We wish to retire soon. I have thought long and hard about an equitable way of anointing my successor. As you know, our lineage has always chosen successors based not just solely on blood relation but rather by choosing one that has proven capability. In that respect, each of my sons and nephews is quite talented and eligible. However, they are not ready to be handed the rule of Ayodhya just yet. I therefore wish to hear from this august Council as to how we can proceed in planning for my eventual succession."

Sage Vasishta was the first to respond in his customary measured voice: "Wise *Ramachandra*," he always addressed Rama with his full name. "This land is our *karma Bhoomi*[7], where we are duty-bound to be attached to it, primarily because of the conduct of your lineage. Centuries ago, your wise ancestor Manu had a vision to go beyond the then pastoral life

---

7   ***Karma Bhoomi*** – Land where one is duty-bound to protect;

and establish a rule based on Dharma. He codified several practices and gave it a structure in his treatise called *Manusmriti*. And according to that treatise, we ought to grow as a society inclusively, rather than forcing our way of life down on other populations. Countless examples of your ancestors that have placed this throne above their own family abound, such as that of *Harishchandra, Dilipa* or *Bhagiratha*. Indeed, some of your ancestors have chosen an outsider from their own family as their successor. Often these lieges have left their own indelible mark to have earned the right to imprint their names in the successor lineage. Hence the rulers of this throne have at various times called themselves the dynasty of *Rishaba, Bharata, Ikshvaku* or *Raghu*. And now, my dear Ramachandra, you have earned this right as well. As you have brought stability, peace, and prosperity without compromising on Dharmic principles, this rule of yours will forever be called Ramrajya, and it will set a benchmark for future dynasties. You are, however, right in thinking about your successor. And the exigent matters that have come to light require you and your brothers' full attention. But before you decide on your successor, why don't you consider performing an *Ashvamedha*[8]ritual,

---

8   *Ashvamedha* – Ancient ritual involving the practice of letting loose a sacrificial horse. The regions it roams would be annexed by the King conducting this ritual. Anyone objecting to this must challenge this King in battle.

just as your father did? This will further cement the sovereignty of Ayodhya. It is perhaps a quicker and cleaner way to expand into territories that are abundant in natural and mineral resources. This will cement your hold on the kingdom while giving security and safety to our people."

Bharata immediately stood up, bowed before Rama and Guru Vasishta and spoke: "I apologize for speaking out of turn, brother. But the wise Guru Vasishta has indeed spoken the truth. Just as our father performed this ritual and just as the four of us, then young, handled the army, performing this ritual now will allow our sons to travel far and wide. And anybody that dares stop the horse shall face our valiant sons in battle."

Although Bharata is typically impetuous, I admit I agreed with him and Guru in this. The Ashvamedha ritual may be expensive, but it is the most efficient and less wasteful of all the other options. Yet I couldn't help but notice that Gurus Vasishta and Rishyasringa exchanged glances and nodded slightly among themselves. Did they agree with each other? If so, when did they meet to discuss? I often wonder if these Rishis can communicate with each other through mind voices.

Sage Rishyasringa got up and spoke: "My dear child Bharata. Your respect for your Guru knows no bounds. I must admit it is a tempting idea. Normally, I would have agreed with that. However, before you decide, let me remind you that the context of your father performing this ritual was different. Three-and-a-half decades ago, the Aryavarta republic had nearly crumbled. This was primarily because Ravana had adroitly created a rift and mistrust between Dravida desa and Bharata Desa. The old Suryavanshi-Chandravanshi clan differences were played up by him through feigned loyalties. Similarly, he ensured the backing of the powerful clans of Haihayas and Sakyas remained on his side

He achieved this by composing his Rudra hymns, which became very popular with wider Nagvanshi people. Those clan leaders had no choice but to support him, as their people are ardent followers of the legendary Lord Rudra, on whom the hymns were based. To top it all, the drought and earthquakes from years prior to that had caused people to migrate out of their traditional homelands of the West and move East or South. Some even went back to the steppe grassland plains up North. It was imperative that King Dasharatha perform the Ashvamedha ritual. I even helped conduct those rituals. However, the context today is different. Using this ritual as a tool only to further the reaches of your suzerainty will be disastrous. The vassals of Kosala will not accept this. Are you prepared for that?

Are your sons ready to handle that? Is that what the sons of Dasharatha fought for?"

After placing such probing questions, he calmly sat. Silence. Bharata and I looked at each other stumped. We were hoping that the Sage would provide solutions rather than ask more questions to this already confounding situation. Yet another trait of these sages – to speak in rhetoric and riddles!

Jambavan stood next and addressed the assembly: "Wise sages and princes, know this. I shall tear to pieces anybody that ever stands in the way of Lord Rama! While I don't see the need for Lord Rama to abdicate the throne, I don't mind all your young sons being given gubernatorial posts that would allow them to get real-world experience. And I shall join you in battling any mleccha foreigner that dares to disturb this Ramrajya, with or without new-age weapons." roared Jambavan. Even at this advanced age, Jambavan retained his gruff voice, gait, and upright stance, thus making him look taller than he is. This gentle giant is full of deserving to be in the Council. You can count on his bravery, positivity, and the enormous confidence he brings to a gloomy environment.

I signaled to Shatrugna to speak next. He took my cue, stood up, bowed before all the members, and then turned to Rama: "Our elders have indeed spoken the truth. While I am pained to hear from my liege, who has been a father figure for me, that he will abdicate the throne soon, I fully realize that our dear lives that we have so taken for granted indeed are nearing their end. As far as I am concerned, I fully endorse the collective wisdom that is present in this august assembly.

In fact, my sons as well as those of Lakshmana's have been raised by our mother Sumitra and our respective wives, in such a manner that they will always be by the sides of their brothers and this throne, and that they will not stake a claim for their share. Above all, I will follow my brothers to wherever they go and complete whatever mission there is yet to finish."

I let Shatrugna speak ahead of me because he is much more erudite and articulate. I tend to be a bit blunt. Nevertheless, I finally rose up and said: "As times are changing, we need to change with the time. I too agree with Sage Rishyasringa and Jambavan to provide leadership roles for our sons. Let them prove their mettle. However, for them to be successful three things must happen. First, we need additional details about possible locations where the young princes can go and establish their base. I trust Hanuman's scouts to have come up with a few options for this. Second, we must guide them for about a year to help them establish their presence and, more importantly, their identity. Third, Rama must be fully authorized to take any decision on choosing his successor."

Rama spoke: "Wise sages, able elder Jambavan, my doting brothers, you have all spoken your minds, and have given structure to the provincial governorship responsibilities to our young princes. Yes, I shall answer some of the questions that were raised here. Thus far, our priorities have been to establish a peaceful kingdom, provide political stability and govern with clear laws of our Dharma. And we have been quite successful in that. However, if our future must be secure, we need to stay ahead of emerging trends. After due consideration, discussion and thought, I wish to propose my vision. The cornerstone of my vision is based on four strategic priorities, namely: Innovation, Commerce, Finance and Education. Thus, the locations we choose to expand must satisfy the following criteria. Each of my brothers will oversee this for some time and eventually transition to their sons: A mining region that supplies raw materials, with workshops situated to experiment with new alloys and develop modern tools and weapons; Lakshmana will head this mission.

A production cluster that has factories and is close to navigable rivers, or on one of our major highways, or better still, by the coast. This can eventually become a trading hub; Shatrugna will oversee setting this up.

A town – possibly very near Ayodhya – that acts as a financial center where merchant guilds can establish their posts and financiers are located; I will personally supervise this.

A center for knowledge and education where various schools of thought exist and where various disciplines of studies can be taught, and perhaps a place that can produce '*Vedas*' or 'Books of Knowledge.' Bharata will lead this mission."

Wah! Rama just outlined a radical vision. The clarity of thought and the boldness of his plans are why Rama was going to be adored for generations to come. Rama then turned to Hanuman, who till then was inconspicuously seated on the far side, gilded gracefully to Rama's side and then held aloft a map that had clear markings of certain regions.

Rama gave a nod to Hanuman, who proceeded to speak: "Respected members of this esteemed Council, based on intelligence input, I have marked potential provinces where our young princes can establish their base. These are remote areas that are self-administered by locals and are mostly left ungoverned by the major Aryavarta kingdoms. Some of them lack resources but have enterprising people. In some, it's the other way around. There are challenges in each of these provinces including proper access, no central economic unity, and diverse racial societies that are often in fractious conflict among themselves. Yet each of them offers excellent opportunities too if you know what you're looking for."

In his typical style, Hanuman provided an excellent narrative on each of these places marked on his map, along with their history, culture, and potential. The discussions went on for some time with questions raised on various points. Hanuman was well prepared to answer all those questions in a convincing manner.

Eventually, we identified provinces aligned with Rama's four strategic priorities. And in consultation with us, we assigned specific areas for each of our sons. Accordingly, Bharat's sons, Taksha and Pushkala, were marked for the provinces of *Takshashila* and *Pushkalavati* near the *Gandhara* region. The university in Takshashila created a center of *Vidya-parishads* that promoted universal learning. This was probably the first in the known world that would thrive for millennia to come.

My sons, Chitrangada and Chandraketu, were assigned to *Karupada* in *Kalinga* and *Chandrakanti* in *Malwa* regions respectively. These were provinces rich in mineral wealth;

Shatrugna's sons, Suvahu and Surasena, the provinces of *Madhupura* and *Vidisha*, respectively.

Madhupura eventually became a busy trading port on river Yamuna and was renamed as Mathura;

Rama's sons, Luv was to govern *Shravasti* in Awadh, and Kush was to govern *Kushavati* – a hard to reach but a beautiful place surrounded by Vindhya mountains. These places were strategically located to attract merchants, craftsmen, and artisans such that both enterprise and finance can thrive.

At the back of our minds, we were thinking if Hanuman's suspicions on Chyavanas and their recent activities were going to hamper our plan. However, Rama was very clear that we proceed with the stated strategic objectives. He believed in building on our strengths rather than fortifying our defense. As more information flows on the Nagvanshi threat, we would handle it at that time. Till then, his order was to proceed with the original plan.

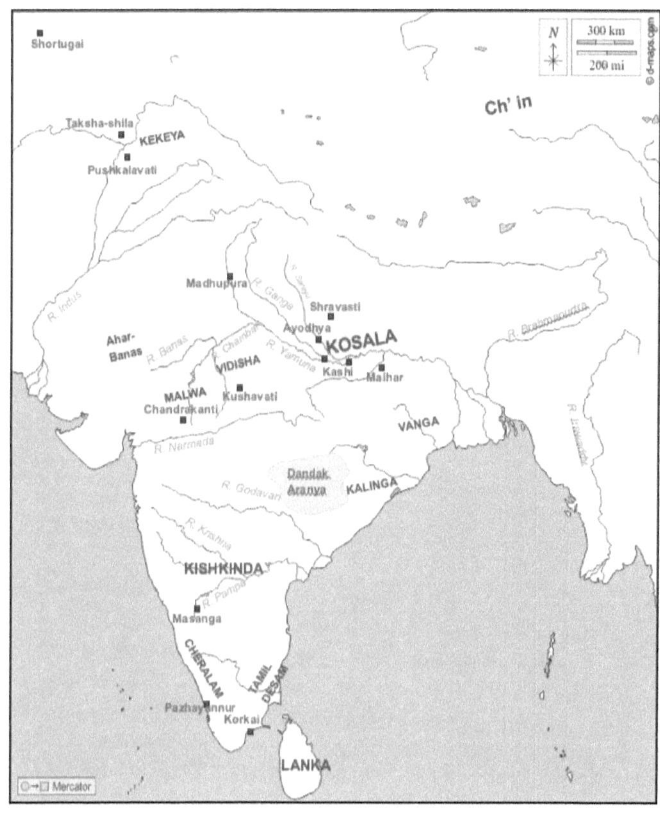
Shortugai
Taksha-shila
KEKEYA
Pushkalavati
Madhupura
R. Ganga
Shravasti
Ayodhya
KOSALA
Kashi
Maihar
Ahar-Banas
R. Banas
Chambal
R. Yamuna
VIDISHA
MALWA
Kushavati
Chandrakanti
VANGA
R. Narmada
Dandak Aranya
R. Godavari
KALINGA
R. Krishna
KISHKINDA
R. Pampa
Masanga
CHERALAM
TAMIL DESAM
Pazhayannur
Korkai
LANKA
Ch' in
R. Brahmaputra
N
300 km
200 mi
Mercator

Part 2 – A Self-Awakening

|| Dharmaatma ||

Chapter 4

Vishwamitra Arrives in Ayodhya

"*Baba*, are you ready? We just heard the royal decree read out, and we rushed over here to come see you," asked an excited Chitrangada. He was accompanied by Chandraketu. My sons, whom Urmila and I affectionately used to call as Angad and Ketu, just arrived in Ayodhya and immediately came to see me in my palace. Even as they entered my chambers, they were quickly followed by their cousins and Rama's sons – Luv and Kush. I embraced the boys warmly. I was hoping to spend more time with my sons and nephews, as I hadn't seen them for nearly a year. There was plenty to talk about but even more to do. The royal decree must have come out even as I was preparing for our trip.

My sons looked a bit stressed by the events that had just occurred over the past month or so. The anticipation around their new assignment outside Ayodhya must have been a bit overwhelming for them to digest. After exchanging initial inquiries about their young brides and their travel coming into Ayodhya, I convinced them I would explain to them later about why a decision was made by Rama to assign responsibilities to each of the young princes at various far-off provinces. As far as my sons were concerned, Angada was tasked with governing Karupada near Kalinga and Ketu was to govern Chandrakanti in Malwa region. But right now, we needed to get ready for our journey ahead, as the monsoons were soon to set in and if it did, that would make our travel that much harder. Accordingly, we prepared for our departure.

My sons and I agreed that we would first go to their maternal grandfather's palace in Kashi city and pay respects to their mother's final resting place. Ever since Urmila passed away, I had grown a bit aloof from my sons. So, in a way, this journey was a good chance for me to reconnect with them, and I was looking forward to that. The boys also warmed up to the idea of taking a trip down to Kashi with me before starting off with their first real leadership responsibilities. Not to be left behind, Luv and Kush too pleaded with me that they come along as well. After all, Kashi was their maternal grandfather's city too. I agreed enthusiastically.

The next day, very early in the morning, the five of us, along with a very few of my bodyguards and assistants, left Ayodhya. Our trip was mostly on a boat, first downstream on River Sarayu sailing South, and then upstream on River Ganga heading West. The summer was almost coming to an end, and the water level in the rivers was low. But this early in the morning, a cool breeze from the river gently beat down on us and it kept me alert. I estimated that it would take five days to reach the ancient holy city of Kashi. This great city was once ruled by the legendary Lord Rudra himself, who went on to earn a god-like status.

I stood on the deck of our ship and looked at the city buildings that were gradually fading away. The morning sun rays were slowly coming up and falling on the copper-plated gates of the fort, making it shine. I looked at my beloved city thinking its future is about to change, only wishing that the change would be for the better. The old rustic idyllic charm is likely to give way to a more dynamic modern city. I have always believed that organic change is good.

"When do you decide whether to go with your gut instinct or not?" I veered around to see the boys standing next to me. I didn't hear them come. They seemed to be in a relatively better mood, although there was a touch of anxiety written on their faces. But as I was lost in my own thoughts, I didn't quite catch the question. "Sorry, come again," I said.

"Say you are faced with a decision. But the choices you are confronted with are those that test your moral code or those that demand exigencies of the greater good?" asked Angad.

"In war, as in politics, Rama's word is my Dharma," I replied without any hesitation, although I wasn't sure what prompted Angad to ask me that.

"Even if that goes against established norms?" Angad followed up.

"Yes. You see, son, I let Rama worry about what is right and what is wrong. His one word is enough for me."

"But while that may have worked in most situations, did it ever bother you to follow his words, even when you know he may have acted in a manner that contradicts Dharma?"

I looked at Angad keenly for a moment and then looked at the other three boys. Then I said, "Son, you seem to have something else in mind. Why don't you ask what you want to ask directly?"

Angad hesitated a bit, but Ketu spoke up: "Father, we mean no disrespect to you, our uncles, or aunts. Rather, we are proud to have been born in this family of greats. In fact, back in our Gurukul, the teachers would use examples from your life to drive home their point. While that is all well for learning, we have now reached a stage where each of us is taking on real-world responsibilities. We are sure to face many such situations that pose a dilemma. We want to be decisive in our decision and at the same time take the right action. Our conduct may at times be in contrast with what we learned. And I am sure that kind of moral dilemma, even you all would have faced. For instance, when Uncle Ram killed Tataka or Vali, was he not worried about going against Raj-Dharma? In the former situation, how did he handle the situation of a Kshatriya prince having to kill a woman in a duel?"

Hmm, my sons have indeed learned well at Guru Vasishta *Vidya-peetam*[9]. The style of teaching at that place is either by asking questions or through storytelling or discerning by way of introspection. I had heard that this branch of study is now gaining popularity at most Gurukuls. They call it *Katha-Upanishad* and *Prasna-Upanishad*. Nevertheless, I felt this was a valid question, one that warranted a convincing explanation.

So, I replied: "Boys, our ancients had codified Dharma to be applied equally for all humanity: whether it's the Rajan, the King, or the praja, the commoner. Thus, a breach of Dharma is a crime and that should

---

9   *Vidya-Peetam* – a higher institution of learning

      Upanishad – sacred texts that add clarity and meaning to the 'Vedas;' **katha** – story; **prasna** – questions

not go unpunished, no matter who the offender is. Our Dharmic laws are well codified to measure the level of punishment. Only a King has the right to pardon a criminal. That too only after considering the contextual and other circumstantial aspects and after consultation with their Priest and the Royal Court.

In fact, since you brought it up, let's take the case of Tataka's death. In that instance, you knew the 'outcome' first, so you questioned the 'act.' I shall recount the story of how and why Tataka was killed. You may be able to judge the 'outcome' differently. You can then interpret if you think the 'act' was according to Dharma or not. Fair?

A little over twenty years ago, your uncles and I had completed our studies and returned back to Ayodhya. There, we were awaiting orders from our father, Emperor Dasharatha, on what our court appointments would be. On one occasion, Rama and I were sent on an errand to investigate a cattle dispute between two villages. On our way back, after completing that matter, we were resting for a bit near River Sarayu, when a messenger came running toward us and said that we were both summoned to the palace immediately. The long winter had finally ended, and spring had begun. The sun was gently beating down. We were lazing around awaiting some real action when we got this word. Sensing something exciting, we quickly got out, dried ourselves, and changed into fresh clothes. The messenger had the good sense to bring us our royal angavastram with our respective insignias embossed on it. After all, you don't enter the palace Assembly Hall without proper attire. We reached there in no time, expecting a full Assembly Hall with the usual hustle and bustle of babbling members. Instead, we saw our father pleading with an elderly stranger."

"Sire! Why do you insist on taking Rama and Lakshmana on this dangerous mission? They have just completed their studies. I have not even given them any administrative or political responsibilities. In fact, I am consulting our astrologers to fix their marriage alliances, as we speak," pleaded our father to that person.

We realized that the impassive-looking gent at the receiving end was none other than the legendary Guru Vishwamitra. Guruji had come unannounced, as had been his wont. A '*Brahmarishi[10]*' like him is accorded elite status anywhere in Aryavarta. Sage Vishwamitra, if you didn't know, was a fearsome-looking tall man, with a rugged beard knotted at the top, thick eyebrows, and lean strong muscles compared to other sages. We had never met him prior to this, although his reputation

---

10   **Brahmarishi** – the highest order of 'Rishi' or Sage who have attained great knowledge; Hindu texts cite 7 such sages; **ji** – an honorific suffix indicating respect;

was well known far and wide. Sages like him are always on a mission. We don't always understand why they do what they do, and we are not allowed to question or reason with them. Invariably, they have their purpose aligned to the greater good of Aryavarta and to extend our way of life to the wider Bharata Desa. In this, they demand absolute submission from the people and even the kings. Our father, despite his status as a king of kings, was no different. Rumor was that my father tried to keep his distance from such personalities as he was always worried that they would place some demands that he may not be able to fulfill. I didn't understand the insecurities behind that, back then. Lord Parasurama was another such personality that our father had avoided in his early years.

But on that day, Guru Vishwamitra seemed to be in no mood to listen to our father's plea nor was he moved a bit. He ignored our father and instead turned toward Guru Vasishta and said: "Vasishta. If this is how I am to be treated, then I shall never set foot in this kingdom again. All I demand is one thing: Send Rama with me for a few months. Alone. Now."

I froze upon hearing this. And I think Rama was more puzzled than shocked. We looked at each other and just shrugged our shoulders. Marriage… Sage Vishwamitra's demand… Rama going alone… and that too immediately. Nothing made sense. I was shocked more so because he was asking only for Rama to be sent with him. I would have been happy to join them, as I had never been away from my brother Rama for even a day till then and was dying to go on an adventure. But as we watched the proceedings quietly from the far end of the hall, one thing was clear. Sage Vishwamitra was very adamant and determined to get his way. Even the normally unflappable Guru Vasishta looked a bit helpless and was casting glances at our father, signaling him to agree.

Finally, our father sighed and said: "Very well, Guruji. In that case, let all my sons accompany you. They have never lived separately for this long. Besides, they all could use your tutelage. Bharata and Shatrugna have gone to their maternal grandfather's place at Kekeya. As soon as they return, I shall send all of them with you. Till then, please honor us by staying here for a few days."

"No, Dasharatha. The mission I have in mind cannot wait. Very well, if only Rama and Lakshmana are here, I shall take them with me. But we must leave immediately," said Vishwamitra firmly.

Since there seemed to be no room for further negotiation, my exasperated father gave in and agreed to send us both to accompany the Rishi. Rama and I were thrilled about finally getting some action.

True, it would have been even more fun had Bharata and Shatrugna also been with us. But we put that thought away, sought blessings from our parents, paid our respects to Guru Vasishta, and then embarked on our journey."

Chapter 5

Battle with Tataka

"The journey itself was intriguing. Sage Vishwamitra was very silent initially. He took us in a South Western direction, avoiding all major routes that merchants typically took. Instead, we kept close to various tributaries of the River Ganga, hiking mostly, and occasionally hitchhiking on small boats. I was amazed at the Rishi's agility, knowledge of the terrain, and forethought. He knew when to take breaks, where there could be food, and at times he seemed to know the boatmen as well. Clearly, he was a frequent traveler in these parts. Upon reaching a place somewhat close to where the River Sarayu joins River Ganga, we were mesmerized by the beauty of the landscape. This was a transformed place full of lush green meadows surrounded by trees of all kinds. There were canopy trees such as Gulmohar, Peepal, Deodars, and aromatic trees such as Parijaat, Sandalwood, and fruit trees such as Mango and Kesar. Against the backdrop of distant mountains, this presented a picturesque break from the path we had been taking. Sage Vishwamitra mentioned that the place was called '*Kama-ashrama*' (or) Kama's grove. Legend has it that Lord Rudra had burned this place that belonged to a social discard Kama and rebuilt a hermitage for learning and meditation. Over time, it had become a rest area for wandering sages and traveling merchants. We stopped at this paradise to rest up, unbeknownst to a problem lurking beneath.

Rama observed something peculiar about this place. He pointed out to the sage about the lack of people at the hermitage. Yes, the place looked somewhat abandoned. We saw very few Rishis and almost no merchants. Rishi Vishwamitra nodded in agreement but asked us to first freshen up, gather some food, and light a fire. Strangely, he asked us to keep our knife, bow, and arrow ready. Anyway, we don't question the sage much. He went up to the nearby stream to wash up and said his evening prayers before coming back to the hut. We had carried some food that was given to us by some Rishis that we met along the way. Having had a decent bite, we settled around the fire, hoping to get the Rishi to tell us about our mission. After a long pause during which he appeared to be keenly focusing his mind on something, and much to our disappointment, the Rishi asked us to retire for the night. Of course, we offered to take turns to stay guard, but he waved us off.

Recognizing the futility of trying to convince him, we both quietly left him by the fire, went to the corridor of a hut, and laid down. He was still seated and meditating where we left him. I think it must have been an instant sleep, for the first thing I noticed was that it was early dawn and Rishi Vishwamitra was standing beside Rama. I noticed a slight smile on his face and a gentle paternal look. Was he silently admiring Rama instead of waking him up? Anyway, I noisily stirred up, greeted the Rishi who, in an instant, went back to his familiar upright stance with a pensive look on his face. He looked at me and then again at Rama, who also woke up, and asked us to get ready and join him in his morning prayers. After we freshened up, we caught up with him again by the stream on the far side of the ashram. There, he taught us a new chant that he had composed, which he called the *Gayatri mantra*, and asked us to recite it every day. After that, as we sat down to eat, he started talking. More like giving commands rather than having a discussion.

He began: "My dear *Kakutstha* Rama and Lakshmana.' Now, no one had ever used that prefix to address us before. 'Kakutstha' was another one of our great ancestors and grandson of Emperor Ikshvaku. So, I was a bit surprised why and how the Rishi used that honorific prefix to address us. I made a mental note to find that out later.

He continued: "I am planning to set up my second ashram here. However, as you noted last night, it is now almost in an abandoned state. This is all due to the capricious *Yakshi* tribe people that are harassing the Rishis or robbing the merchants that pass by here."

"Guruji, can the local chieftain or even the king not do something about it? It's a shame that such a beautiful place is nearly abandoned," asked Rama.

"Yes, they can, but they won't. The local chieftains are either in the payroll of the Yakshis or too afraid of them," replied the sage.

"Surely, they can see the folly of letting these Yakshas have a free run. After all, they lose out on the tax income that they could have otherwise collected from the merchants," asked Rama, pressing the point further.

The sage guffawed and said: "As the chieftains and possibly the local inspectors are themselves in cahoots with the tribe, they won't report these things."

Rama seemed perturbed by this and after a few moments asked: "Guruji. What can we do to help?"

Sage Vishwamitra smiled a bit, as if he was expecting Rama to ask exactly that question, and said: "For now, nothing much. I want you both to take a post each at the outer boundaries of this ashram and observe. I have some work to do here. Do not react or expose yourselves, even if anything happens. Meet me here exactly after a week."

As direct an order as can be, and as vague an objective as there is. The frustrating part of dealing with Sage Vishwamitra is that he won't tell you anything till he has to. Anyhow, we felt this mission was still better than doing nothing back in Ayodhya. So, Rama and I quickly conferred on where and how we would lay in ambush and what kind of traps we should set. We needed to pick a spot that gave us a good view of who was coming and going out of the ashram. At the same time, it shouldn't reveal our hideout. After some scouting, I picked two spots, some short distance away from each other. It was close enough for us to communicate through bird calls. I picked two peepal trees, one for each of us. This gave us enough cover, and the branches were wide enough for us to be seated. We then dug a series of small pits all around the place and covered them with some twigs. As the spring was upon us, there weren't too many dry leaves. But we made do with what cover we could find in order to make it look natural. Of course, the peepal trees in that area gave us plenty of vines for us to set some traps. While we did not know what or who we were looking for, nor how long that would take, we were hoping that we could spot a danger if we saw something unusual. At the very least, whoever or whoever came should alert us based on the sounds they might make when they crossed this path. Easier said, I suppose. What happened over the next five days was just an unbelievable turn of events for which we were not prepared at all."

I took a pause in my narration and had some fruit and nuts that Angad had quietly slipped next to me, which I washed down with some milk. I was expecting some reaction from my sons, but they were just silently sitting without moving or blinking. I guess they must have enjoyed hearing about my adventures. Finally, Angad broke the silence and asked in a gasping voice: "Father, did the Guru Vishwamitra come back to the place or did he just abandon you? And did the tribal attack you?"

I couldn't help but chuckle and replied: "Did Guruji come back? Well, let's see.

Days 1 – 3: Rama and I waited and waited. Nothing much really happened, save for a stray mendicant that came, stayed for a night, and left.

Day 4: Guruji came back with his retinue of students in the afternoon. They each carried basic needs for their accommodation and materials for their rituals. It clearly looked like they were settling down here. However, since the Rishi had strictly told us not to interfere for a week, we were both lying quietly and watching the proceedings.

Day 5: Rishi Vishwamitra and his disciples had cleaned and prepared the place to conduct what looked like a massive yagna, or fire ritual. I have never seen one directly, although it is well known that your grandfather, King Janaka, was famous for conducting these yagnas often.

Day 6: At the crack of dawn, the Rishi and a few of his senior disciples started the yagna. It was also Amavasya, i.e., 'no-moon day,' considered auspicious to start any ritual. By this time, I was done with all this watching. I was exhausted, as was Rama. My joints and muscles were aching from being holed up on a tree branch and catching up a few winks here and there. I was looking forward to going back to the ashram the next day.

The whole day they had some rituals or the other. I didn't quite follow, but the entire place was reverberating with their chants. That calmed my mind. We were taught some of this at our Gurukul and I'm sure even you boys might have learned some. The *anustubh* and the *tristubh*[11] metres are some of the oldest rhythmic patterns and listening to them for some

---

11   **Anustubh and tristubh** – Respectively 8 and 11 syllables (or Chanda) in a poetic stanza. These are two of the most commonly used metres in the composition and chanting of Rig Veda, Valmiki Ramayana, Gayatri mantra, and several shlokas.

time is meditative. I felt like even the birds and the grazing deer were mesmerized by the chanting.

They finally ended the day's ritual with the customary *sandya vandanam* or the 'evening sun prayers.' I was glad that the rituals went well without any interruption or disturbance. I was thinking to myself that perhaps this whole disruption thing associated with the Yakshas was just some myth? I gave a pre-agreed bird call to Rama, conveying that all was clear at my end and that I was ready for the first watch. I got a return acknowledgment bird call from him as well. I could make out that the fire embers were gradually fading. It looked like the Rishi and his disciples must have slept off. It was quiet for a while. That day being Amavasya, naturally, the night was pitch dark. Well, as you can imagine, sitting atop a peepal tree on such a day can test the bravest of men. And I was just a young lad – about your age back then. And I was exhausted after six days of lying in ambush with heightened senses. So, it is fair to say my eyelids were starting to droop a bit.

No sooner had I almost dozed off than I heard a 'whoosh' sound. Actually, a pair of them. I woke up with a start but saw nothing. I thought it must have been the bats. They must have been attracted to the bugs and other small rodents that could've crept up near the yagna fireplace – what with small remains of ghee, rice, jaggery, and vegetable scraps lying about. Then suddenly another pair of whoosh sounds. And then after a few minutes another pair. I was fully alert by then.

These noises sounded much heavier, a tad bit slower but coordinated, than what bats would make. Then a few minutes later, I heard a wild scream. It was coming from the hut. I couldn't make out as the fire from the yagna pit was almost thinning out. Then more noises. I made a quick bird call to Rama and got down. I lied low, crouched behind trees and bushes, and went near the huts. I could make out Rama's silhouette by the far side. The noises were cries for help. I saw the priests and students running out. By now I could make out that they were also injured. There was some melee. I could not see where Guru Vishwamitra was. But I saw dark-skinned, scantily dressed folks covered with ashes and wearing masks. They had long, flowing, red-dyed hair or maybe a wig made of coconut coir. The masks, along with their ash-covered skin and long, flowing red hair on a no-moon night with minimal light from the fire, made them look very intimidating and scary. If they wanted to create these special effects, they couldn't have chosen a better night and a better costume. But I was wondering who they were and what they wanted. They didn't seem to kill anyone, thankfully. They were, however, ransacking the place, causing a bedlam and generally shouting and making strange sounds. There were about two dozen of them. Rama and I decided to attack, and we used our swords and spears to fight them. Although it was all chaotic, there was some method to their madness. First, they were well trained to fight. Secondly, they were well coordinated. They came in waves of two at a time. Each pair would run toward us, parry with their spears and clubs, and then run away. Then the next pair came and repeated this. And so on. Each time from a different direction. I realized that their aim was to tire us out and capture us all alive. Rama and I decided to fight with our backs rubbing each other's, so as not to give them a chance to injure us. This way, we could face them in all directions. But we were wondering who their leader was, coordinating these attacks, although there seemed to be a lady or ladies among them shouting orders. We couldn't make out the voices clearly nor understand their language but placed it as some dialect of Dakshin Bharat. What were our Southern neighbors doing this far North? That didn't make any sense. Meanwhile, the huts started to burn. Looked like these folks were setting the ashram on fire. We could hear the Sage Vishwamitra yelling, "Rama, kill them." Well, that's what we were trying to do, but these sneaky tribals had a way of charging at us like monkeys. Yes, monkeys. They were hopping, dancing, swerving, crouching, suddenly leaping all in a smooth fluidic motion.

And remember, the lighting was poor, so we couldn't make out anyone until they came close to us. Rama and I have never faced enemies fighting this way. So, none of our sword swings hit them well, although we were able to cause injury to a few. Finally, Rama said: "Lakshmana, I've had enough of this circus. I have a plan. Let's double back to our hideouts. We'll lure them to the pits. We may stand a chance if we hear them, even if we can't see them clearly." Brilliant. We both imitated their movements by rolling on the ground. We split up and quickly ran to our hideout trees. Along the way, we dragged a couple of Guruji's students, asking them to go with us without making any noise. Of course, we didn't tell them that they were the bait. Anyway, this seemed to have done the trick. The Yakshas gave us the chase. Rama and I quickly hid behind trees, with a student each keeping close to us. Even if we couldn't see the Yakshas, we would clearly hear them if they stepped on the trap pits. Sure enough, we started hearing thuds, rustles, ooh's and aah's. We felt that was enough, for as soon as we heard a sound, we would club them or poke them with our spear to maim them. Some of them also got caught in our tree vine knots. Killing was a last resort. One by one, we caught most of them. Even some of the Rishi's disciples that came with us assisted by tying the tribespeople up. Since not all of them chased us, we knew this lot wasn't all of them. Also, considering how well they were organized, only a few of them would have been given the orders to go after us. Since the tribals on our side were tied up, Rama and I decided to head back to the main ashram area to subdue the remaining Yakshas. As we came closer, we could still hear Guruji continuing with his shouting and asking Rama to kill them. Was Guruji deliberately mentioning Rama's name aloud for the Yakshas to hear? This went against the cardinal rule of any attack against an unknown enemy where we don't call each other's real name. Guruji was once a king himself and surely, he must know this rule. Well, I'll worry about that later, for I had other things to worry about then. Since the huts were burning, we could make out more clearly who was who. We spotted two individuals not wearing masks. We guessed that they were some sort of leaders. So, we took aim with our bow and arrow to finish them off. At the same time, they too spotted us and, turning toward our direction, started charging at us. Once again, that swerving, leaping motion that made us miss our mark more than once. I caught one of them in his thigh. He fell, cried out in pain and then quickly rolled behind a tree. Rama was giving chase to the other person. And guess what? It was a lady! But by the time they were near enough for us to see clearly, Rama was already firing his arrows in multiple sequences, some of which hit her. She didn't stop and instead kept running toward Rama. By this time, I too came closer toward them, hoping to help Rama. I tried to aim at her but couldn't get a mark. With no other way out, Rama fired a shot at the lady, aiming for her legs, hoping to incapacitate her. But just then she tripped on something and took a fall. The arrow found its mark on her chest, and she fell with a thud, crying out in pain."

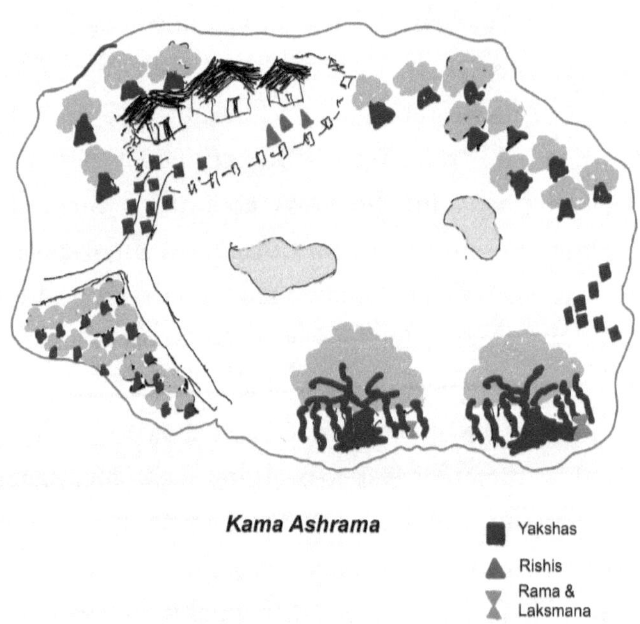

Kama Ashrama

I stopped and paused here. Clearly, the four boys were listening to this narration from the edge of their seats. Angad almost whispered: "Baba, was that Tataka? And did she die?"

I replied: "Yes, son. Rama was looking to incapacitate her, but fate killed Tataka."

"What did Uncle Rama do next? Was he saddened on account of killing a woman? Did Guruji offer some solace?" asked Ketu.

"Solace? By then Guruji and his disciples had rounded up the remaining tribals and tied them up. He came up to us, and his tall frame shook with mirth. He congratulated us for defeating the Yakshas and thanked Rama for killing the Yakshi. I understood then why he kept referring to them as Yakshis. These men were not even tribals. They were from Lanka and were led by this lady Tataka, assisted by her sons Subahu and Mareecha. Mareecha alone escaped while the other two died. They were relatives of the Lanka King Ravana. Their mission was to establish a Lankan outpost by converting this ashram. Ravana used his old links with the lineage of Lord Rudra to stake claim to this ashram but had been opposed by the other Rishis. Hence he resorted to this subterfuge and harassment. 'If I cannot have it, I will ensure no one else can,' seemed to have been his logic. But instead of directly committing his men, he used the Yaksha tribes to achieve his objective. So yes, we had a big grouse to eliminate this threat.

Despite all this, I was quite mad, for I was sure Guruji knew all along who these people were and what would happen to them. I felt like we got tricked into killing a lady, especially since it was against the warrior code to kill a woman. And by shouting Rama's name repeatedly he ensured that anyone hearing all this commotion would clearly know and remember his name. Rama was looking down and avoided looking at Guruji. I know his mind. When he gets angry, he becomes quieter, and his jaw tightens, and he just focuses on some distant object while controlling his breath. Rama must have felt guilty of a crime that he didn't willfully commit."

"I cannot imagine what Uncle Ram would have gone through with his feelings. But what happened next, father?" Ketu continued with his questions.

"You see, Rama's strength is his ability to evaluate all situations with equanimity and logic while staunchly staying within the rules of Dharma. Even at that young age, those traits were very apparent. The details such as their identity, motive and training came to light later. At that time, however, Rama and I were trying to prevent their attacks. During the attack, he noted that these attacks were not sinister. They were mostly harassing the Rishi and his disciples. While engaging them, we found that Tataka was their leader. Despite our Guru yelling at us to kill them, Rama kept aiming for her shoulders and legs. I took a cue from him and aimed at Mareecha's hands.

After the end of this skirmish – I would not call it a battle – Rama tried to take stock of his actions. First, we rounded up all Tataka's men, tied them up, and took them to a nearby military outpost. Guru Vishwamitra's reputation was well known, so they took our prisoners and promised to investigate and act. Even though we suspected that they would be let go eventually, that didn't matter. At least, since their leaders were dead, they wouldn't trouble this ashram again for some time. Over the next three days, we helped clean the ashram and settle Guruji's disciples. After that, Guruji asked us to accompany him. We did as advise. A day's trek and we were in the ashram of Rishi Gautama and Rishi Ahalya."

Chapter 6

Rama Meets Sage Ahalya

"Sons, you must have heard the reputation of Rishi Gautama and his wife Rishi Ahalya. Both the sages have compiled, codified, and promulgated several of our ancient texts and contributed immensely to the *Dharma Shastras* – or 'codified law manual' – that we still use today. Our meeting with these sages made a telling impact on both Rama as well as Sage Ahalya. Before I explain that, I must tell you the backstory to this wise couple. It is said that, once, Sage Gautama suspected his wife of infidelity. This was later proved to be untrue, however. But for several years, she had to live with that stigma. This all started when someone visited their ashram especially when Sage Gautama was away, and this person had claimed to be one of the direct descendants of Lord Indra himself. The family of Lord Indra holds a special status in our society, as you know. Thus, Lady Ahalya welcomed this person as per custom and personally attended to his needs.

This person, however, took advantage of the situation and misbehaved with her. Lady Ahalya was more than capable of handling this situation and, through her intellect and bravery, chased him out. Later, when Sage Gautama came and heard about the incident, he became suspicious of his wife. Instead of finding out the truth, he blamed her for the incident.

Lady Ahalya was infuriated and was so shocked with anger and shame. The residents of that ashram and nearby village too sided with Sage Gautama. All this paralyzed her and she went into a coma, becoming almost stone-like. Eventually, she recovered, but the mental scar remained. This tense situation continued even at the time when we visited their ashram. While reaching their place, Sage Gautama accorded a warm welcome to Rishi Vishwamitra. Ahalyaji was subdued in her reception. Both sages conversed by exchanging their experiences and knowledge gained over the years. It appeared as if they knew each other but were meeting after a long time. Rama and I, of course, kept mostly quiet during this whole discussion. After our initial introduction, Ahalyaji went inside their hut. I assumed that she needed to take care of meals and other chores. After some time, during the discussion between the sages, Guru Vishwamitra asked Rama and me to go and help Lady Ahalya. A welcome change, indeed, from a conversation, half of which we didn't understand.

Now, the situation inside the hut was also a bit uncomfortable for us. Ahalyaji neither acknowledged our presence nor did she respond much to our offer of helping her. So, Rama and I tried our best to find something to help with.

Several minutes went like this. Finally, she said: "They say you are different." This she said without even looking at us. Neither of us knew who she was talking to, nor what the context was. Rama politely asked: "Ahalyaji, were you speaking to us?" She replied: "Do you see anyone else here?" That was unnerving. Ahalyaji was a great scholar and had a reputation for speaking very little. So, if you speak some gibberish, it might irritate her. Alternatively, if you didn't latch on to the very few words she speaks, then you miss out on pearls of wisdom. While physically she was weak, mentally she was very sharp. Rama tried his luck one more time. I was happy to play the part of keeping my mouth shut. He asked: "We are here as students of Brahmarishi Vishwamitra. So, we are happy to oblige him in any way he commands us."

"And yet, you hesitated in killing Tataka." That bolted out of nowhere, catching us off guard. Rama kept quiet. She continued: "A future King cannot be conflicted in his thoughts. You would be forced to take a split-second decision on a battlefield. And then you cannot second-guess those decisions from the comforts of your ivory throne later."

I surely did not follow this line of thought at that time. Thankfully, Rama seemed to have. He carefully responded: "Our Dharmic laws are clear in that type of situation. What I saw in front of my eyes was someone that was out to destroy our way of life. That it was a woman did not matter."

She continued to repeat: "Yet, you hesitated."

Rama clarified his point as: "Even if it were a man, I would have looked to neutralize them, not kill them. Especially since they did not try to kill us. I decided based on facts, not emotions."

She changed her line to: "Yet, you seem to feel a sense of guilt. And that guilt caused you to hesitate. Why Rama?" Rama kept quiet and did not respond. She continued: "Shall I tell you why? You were feeling guilty for other people's actions. You were wondering why your own Guru was asking you to kill her. Not just that. You were thinking of a similar incident that concerned your father a few years before you were born, were you not? That's right. You were thinking of that day when Emperor Dasharatha was on a hunting trip somewhere near that same Kama-ashrama and he accidentally killed an unarmed boy, named Yagnadatta. That boy was just getting some water to provide to his blind parents. Yet, in the darkness, Emperor Dasharatha thought it was a deer that he heard and killed the boy by mistake. Ever since, he has carried that guilt. And you were too. Thus, when your arrow found its mark on Tataka's chest instead of her legs, you had the same feeling as that of your father. In fact, it was that guilt feeling that caused your aim to falter. Surely, a great archer such as yourself could have easily adjusted your grip even when you saw Tataka trip and fall. Tell me if I am wrong!"

I was shocked that this otherwise reticent Lady Ahalya laid bare the innermost feelings of Rama. He had tears rolling down his eyes, confirming my fear that he concurred with her assessment. How could Ahalyaji be so stone-hearted? I admit I didn't realize he carried such feelings inside, while battling Tataka. But I didn't understand why that should bother him so much or why he must carry such guilt.

Rama fell at Ahalyaji's feet, held them tight and cried out. This was the first time, as far as I knew, that Rama even cried. Anyone in that position would have done the same.

He pleaded: "Ahalyaji, was what I did forgivable? Did I commit a blunder in killing Tataka? Will the same curse that my father faced after his error also haunt me?"

Ahalyaji gently caressed his head, lifted him up, wiped his tears and touched his chin. Her eyes glistened slightly, which she wiped and then said in a very affectionate tone: "My child. Don't worry. I didn't mean to point out all this to make you feel guilty. On the other hand, my aim was to relieve you of any blot that you think you have. Tataka deserved to die. It is her fortune that it was in your hands. She has driven many a Rishis and traveling merchants to commit suicide or die of fear. She tortured and harassed innocent people and ensured that no one stayed at Kama-ashrama. The crimes she and her sons have committed are far beyond justification. Her methods were crueler than a simple stab in one's stomach.

That she happens to be a woman is of no consequence. In fact, I am happy that you have not used gender as a point of consideration. Your Guruji knows that too. This is an important aspect you should always remember. Emotions can cloud judgment. As a future leader, you must learn to deal with the facts at hand and not bring in other events that have no bearing on that particular incident. What your father did was an honest mistake. He tried to make up for it as best as he could. Many people in that instance would have escaped from that place instead of facing the problem. Your father, Emperor Dasharatha, did not do that. He owned up to his mistakes. Similarly, you were dealt to handle a situation. You are young. You have to listen to your Guru, and he advised you to act. Yet, you deliberated on it as long as possible and finally, you finished the job. But once you complete a task, you must learn to walk away from that action. Any further deliberation would only confuse you.

In fact, I shall teach you a mantra that will help you in maintaining your focus and training your thoughts on the goal at hand. Control the five senses, and you control your destiny. Ramachandra, my child, in future too you shall encounter such moral dilemmas. Life does not always give you dichotomous choices. That is why we have Dharma. Understand this Dharma well, abide by it always. May the almighty protect you and your clan."

So saying, Lady Ahalya walked out of the room gracefully to join the Rishis. I was left blinking at her first, then at Rama and again at her. I could make out from that distance that Guruji nodded at Ahalyaji and had a smile on his face.

Even today, as I think about that incident, I understand that Guruji had anticipated this all along. He probably wanted Rama to go through this experience and meet this great lady. That probably completed his schooling. In fact, this prepared Rama when he faced similar, if not the same, challenges later in his life. There were instances such as, the time he killed Kishkinda King Vali, not in a direct duel but rather pairing with Vali's brother Sugreeva, or when he killed Lanka King Ravana, who was a Brahmin. On both occasions, Rama did not let moral compunctions interfere with his thinking. He operated with a simple mantra: 'All transgressions on Dharma must be put down and the oppressors must be punished as deemed by our Samhita.' Their social, gender or class identity is not relevant, in the eyes of law."

Angada and Ketu listened to this action-packed story that was full of moral values, leadership tidbits, emotions and above all reiteration of values. After this, there were no further questions, as I knew their earlier questions on Dharma and values were clarified. They stood staring at the distant horizon. Their own future awaits them. They probably had thoughts of what they will be known for, what challenges they will face and how they will handle all that.

Part 3 – The Oppressed Turn the Tables

|| Sitamma Mayamma ||

Chapter 7

Lakshmana's Discourse with Luv and Kush

It was late afternoon by the time we reached Kashi city. Word of our arrival must have been sent ahead, for we were welcomed by the palace royals, musicians, priests and a few common folks. Before the arrival of the monsoons, the city comes alive in vibrant colors and wears a joyful atmosphere. The pristine waters of Ganga turned cooler and wafted a gentle breeze mixing with the warm sun rays, making the whole atmosphere pleasant. The smell of incense, flowers, lamps and sandal paste filled the air with an aroma.

I was reminded of the first time Rama and I came here, brought by Guru Vishwamitra after Sita bhabhi's *'swayamvar'* – a competition that was held for eligible princes and kings of that time, where the most ideal suitor wins princess Sita as his bride, based on winning that competition. Rama, of course, easily won that competition and along with it won the hand of Sita bhabhi. The competition was held in Mithila, but after the marriage, we came to Kashi first as this was a holy city and a center of learning. Since my marriage with Urmila was also held at the same time in Mithila, we too accompanied Rama and Sita bhabhi. I was reminded of the same atmosphere prevailing even today, but my mind was elsewhere. I wanted to head straight to the outskirts of the city and went to the "*Mithila putri vana.*" This referred to the 'Garden of daughters of Mithila,' who were Sita and Urmila. My nephews and sons were keen to join me to get there, pay respects to the memorial fireplace of their respective mothers and generally enjoy the surroundings of that garden. The citizens of Kashi kept a flame in the fireplace always burning.

Luv came up to me and said "Uncle, thank you for allowing us to accompany you here. Truth be told, we were hoping to spend time with you, talk to you and learn from you. You were the only one that used to visit us when we were at the Valmiki ashram, in our youth. We always looked forward to meeting you. And now it appears that we may not see you for a long time, possibly never."

"Sons, I too wanted to spend time with you all. And I have so much to talk about and yet words fail me. Well, we are here together for a few days, aren't we? Why don't we make the most of it? Ask me about something that's at the top of your mind, which you wish to know. I can spend some time this evening," I said.

That calmed them a bit and Kush asked: "Lakshman Chacha, on our return to Ayodhya a few days back, Luv and I were just talking about how much we miss our mother Sita. We were quite young when we were growing up at Guru Valmiki's ashram. And for a long time, we didn't know that our father was King Rama. Mother raised us all by herself. But you spent a lot of time with both our parents. You know both better than most. Can you tell us something about our mother Sita from her past? We are more intrigued by so many legends surrounding our mother. Take for example this garden here in Kashi with her memorial, although she was the princess of Mithila. Or for that matter, we saw some tribal women from Dakshin Bharat come every year to Ayodhya and bring mud idols of our mother, make wooden lamp boats and let them float in the Sarayu River. We saw them a few days back there. That intrigued us."

I looked at Luv and Kush for a few moments, and then gave out a faint smile. "Ah, that brilliant mind of the *devi*. The simplicity with which she can untangle any tricky situation…," I mused.

"There have been numerous instances where your mother has gone out of her way to help women, children and poor people in various aspects. That is why the common folk worship her. The women you saw in Ayodhya are not just from any tribe. They are from the fierce, independent Koitor tribe from Dakshin Bharat. They come every year to perform a ritual in honor of your mother Sita. They make clay replicas of Sita bhabhi. As you can see, they place these dolls on small wooden boards, light a lamp and place them on the Sarayu River to float. To tell you about this ritual, I must take you back in time.

Back then, as you know, our fourteen-year exile took us far and wide. Far, more than wide. We believed that the spirits of our ancestors, especially Sagara and Manu, resided in the Southern part of our great land. So, Rama felt it would be a good yatra to travel up to the vast oceans of Dakshin Bharat. We consulted a few Rishis as well, who advised us that we should be paying our respects and spending our time knowing more about the lands."

"But how did you know where to go, Uncle?" asked Luv.

"We didn't," I said as a matter of fact. "You see, my boy, once you enter the Dhandak forest, you are at its mercy. By the fourth year of our exile, we had mastered basic survival skills, but nothing prepares you for Dhandak forest. The dense foliage doesn't allow much movement. So, we followed along the great river Godavari. And once we entered the kingdom of Asmaka, we decided to camp on the border and plan our next course."

"Asmaka? The one ruled by the legendary King Paudanya? Did you meet him? Was he as terrifying as we have heard, Uncle?" questions poured again from Kush.

"You see, my lad, Rama was very particular about avoiding major roads or towns to avoid revealing our identity," I answered, skipping the question on King Paudanya. "Rama knew that if word of our identity reached any of the local kings or merchants, that would affect the terms of Kaikeyi. We didn't know whom to trust then. Besides, Kaikeyi's terms were for us to live as hermits for fourteen years." I couldn't help rolling my eyes, for the boys glanced at each other. They obviously knew I addressed Queen Mother Kaikeyi just by her name. They must have sensed that my anger against her had not subsided even after all these years.

I averted their glances and continued, "Anyway, just at the border of Asmaka, we built a small hut near the banks of river Godavari and decided to stay there for a few days. It was after the rainy season and the great river was flowing in abundance. I knew we could be self-sufficient for a while just by hunting and eating wild fruits."

"When we go hunting, we take turns to go on first watch to gather our prey. Did you and Uncle Ram do that as well?" asked Kush innocently.

I guffawed. "Bhabhi always set the trap at night, and she always woke up first! And good thing too."

My nephews, Luv and Kush, smiled at a rare admission of weakness from me. They knew that after their aunt Urmila passed away, I had been keeping some distance from my sons and nephews. So, we have not had such a heart-to-heart conversation in several years. Possibly a welcome change felt by both parties.

"Usually, when we woke up, bhabhi would have already picked fruits and herbs for our morning meal. The only thing I was good at was to light a fire. No matter how wet the logs were, I could find a way to get a fire started."

I suddenly stopped and felt my eyes glistening. Another first. Ah! I must not show weakness. Too late, for the boys noticed.

"Are you okay, Uncle?" asked Kush gently.

"To think that it is I who had to light a fire for that great devi, so she could walk on it and prove her purity...," my voice choked.

I was recollecting the painful event in Lanka after the war. Rama finally got to meet Sita bhabhi at the Ashoka van after defeating Ravana. It was meant to be a sweet reunion. Why did Rama have to listen to some charlatan? Why did he agree to have her go through *Agni pariksha* – the ancient custom of proving one's worth by crossing the fire?

"Uncle, please have some water," said Kush.

After a few sips, I composed myself and continued, "One morning, Sita bhabhi brought some strangers to our hut. A young girl and an older lady, who must be her mother. I sensed trouble and instinctively grabbed a knife and started to inquire about them. Rama, as usual, was unflustered. He saw that they were timid, weak and exhausted. They looked like they had been traveling for several days without food. He gave a signal to Sita bhabhi. But even before she could speak, the older lady broke down, fell on bhabhi's legs and begged her to save them."

"What language did they speak, and did you understand that?" asked Kush.

"Not fully. We too were perplexed. It sounded like a Dravida bhasha – language of Dravida land – although I couldn't clearly follow their dialect. However, bhabhi seemed to respond in the universal language of affection. That calmed the lady. The little girl seemed to understand our language and spoke a little. Meanwhile, I sheathed my knife back and offered them some fruits and water. Rama sensed that bhabhi had hit a connection with them, and he was happy to let her speak for the most part. The amazing thing about your father is that he can go for a long time without saying anything and yet be at the center of action."

"The girl introduced herself as Sara and her mother as Nagamma. They belonged to the Koitor tribe from a village. As is common with most tribals, they only have first names. They had been running for three days without a break. When enquired, Sara said they were escaping from King Paudanya's soldiers and were taking her mother to the other side of the river. 'Why them?' I asked. Apparently, the soldiers were harassing their village and taking the children as slaves and committing other atrocities on the womenfolk. Sara had escaped with her mother. Once she settled her mother in safety, she was going to return and fight the soldiers. I seethed in anger hearing this and asked what the village men were doing. Apparently, this time of the year after the monsoons was usually best for hunting. All the men go into the forest to gather as much meat as possible and come back after several days. This food sustains them during winter. The king's soldiers learned of this and, like cowards, attacked the villages during this time.

Rama became tense and his jaw tightened. I too was red in anger and was clenching my fist. Even now I feel disgusted by the cowardliness of the Asmakans. But at that time, words escaped me. I mostly hissed and puffed. I had a flowing mane and my face turned red immediately in anger. In fact, my brothers would tease me that I looked like a lion roaring after a kill." I stopped, sensing I was digressing a bit. The story was about Sita bhabhi, not me. I paused for a bit to see if the boys had any questions.

"But why would they attack some villages in their own territory?" asked Luv.

"Slaves and workers. Practical economics. This was Asmaka's main source of income," I said, returning to my 'matter of fact' style of speaking. "Asmaka is blessed with the mighty river Godavari and its tributaries, making the land fertile. Equally significant is also the abundance of precious items such as gold, diamonds and copper. That is why Paudanyapura, their capital, is a busy river port and well connected both inland as well as to the Vanga ocean in the East. Asmaka has trade with several kingdoms beyond our borders. They need laborers, boatmen, peddlers, cooks and all other skilled and unskilled help who make this trade and commerce thrive.

Anyway, even as Sara was narrating their travels, I was looking at Rama to see if he had made any plans to drive out the soldiers. I had some questions in mind about the number of soldiers, their cantonment location, where they sourced their food, and how they transported it."

"Are they still behaving that way, Uncle?" asked Luv.

"Not after your mother taught them a lesson," I said.

"Sita maa?" asked the surprised boys in unison.

"Yes, Sita maa. As I said, she already established a trust with the family. She offered to go with Sara and assess the situation. I jumped at this suggestion and argued that I could go out with Rama and possibly "take care of the situation". I was aware of the risk of doing that, but equally so, I was worried that the Asmaka soldiers might harm or worse capture bhabhi along with the villagers. No, I firmly tried to argue against her plan. But strangely Rama seemed to go along with her plan. He agreed that bhabhi and Sara should go back to the village in secret. Rama and I would cover the flanks at a distance to look for any signs of the soldiers. Nagamma would stay at the hut. It was agreed that we would meet back at the hut in five days. But before leaving, Nagamma finally spoke. We didn't understand a word, but she gave one of her pendants and one of her bangles to bhabhi. She kept addressing her as Janakamma. Rama and I wondered for a moment if this lady knew of our identities. But her eyes exhibited gratefulness and the words came from her heart. I put aside my thoughts and focused on the mission. You could say that I was itching for some action, especially since our first four years had been relatively peaceful, save for a stray dacoit or three that had to be put down."

Chapter 8

Sita Goes on a Reconnaissance Mission

———◆◆———

"Uncle, are you saying mother went and defeated the soldiers? What 'lesson' were you referring to earlier?" asked Luv.

Old age seemed to have made me keep losing focus. I was wandering off my thoughts frequently. Luv reminded me of young Rama. Always steadfast and knew of priorities. Kush takes after Sita bhabhi. Empathetic, calm, and thinks about issues that most people would miss. Yes, the future of Ayodhya is in safe hands, I thought to myself.

"Well, as agreed, we all met back at the hut safely on the fifth day. Let me tell you the remaining part of this story through Sita bhabhi's words. You will understand her better."

Rama: "Vedavati, your eyes tell me that your mission was successful?"

Simple one-liner as always. Conveyed his love and concern for Sita bhabhi while staying focused on the mission. Also, whenever we were in the presence of strangers, we addressed each other with our household names. We didn't want to reveal our royal identity. Sita was Vedavati. I was Anuja – the shadow. And well, we never really called my brother by his name, so I don't even know what his household name was!

Sita: "That and more." She toyed with him a bit. There was more she didn't say than what she said.

I arched my eyebrow, took a stance of an investigating officer, and noted that: "Bhabhi, you and Sara have returned exactly how you went. You haven't brought anyone else nor are you carrying any weapons. I don't see any signs of a fight. Sara seems more relaxed. Clearly, you've either outwitted the soldiers or saved the village womenfolk. Come on, sister! Stop with your teasing. Tell us all."

Sita: "Fairly observant, my dear *devarji*. Is there anything else you can deduce?"

I muttered something about her going on about observation and deductive reasoning, but instead continued: "Before going from here, you left behind all your jewels with Rama, and yet you are now carrying a few jewels including some made from shells. That means you met someone important in the Koitor tribe. And that would have happened only when you were given hospitality and care. Your quiver is still full of arrows, which means you didn't use your bow. Your knife is dull but not chipped, perhaps used for hunting food. Okay, I give up bhabhi. I don't know what really happened there!"

Nagamma, who was watching all this, finally laughed out loud. As I saw all the faces in the room, it looked like everyone but me knew what really happened. I looked away embarrassed.

Sita: "Very good! Well, almost right, Anuja. Yes, we made good time enroute their village. We used a tree log that had fallen during the monsoons as a boat and used that to go down the river. Lastly we trekked up to reach the village. On the outskirts of the village, there were girls with spears perched up on the trees. I probably didn't get killed because of Sara. She made all the correct hand signals to get us in. I was impressed with their silent relay communication that helps them defend their village. These women and girls were quite amazing. I met up with the village matron – Nagamma's cousin – and introduced myself along with our mission. The Asmaka soldiers had somehow figured out the Koitor tribe practice where the menfolk go out hunting during this season. They tried to capture the womenfolk and use them either as slaves or as hostages for the men to surrender and work as slaves in Paudanyapura. They first entice these women.

When that doesn't work, they threaten them. When that too fails, they attack them, burn their houses, and then kidnap the children. The women wailed while narrating these horrific acts. But they still had fire in them. They didn't give up that easily. Most of them are trained in some martial arts and carry weapons such as knives, spears, and poison darts and know how to adapt animal traps as a defensive mechanism. What they seemed to lack is obviously leadership, organization, and fighting techniques for a sustained period."

As bhabhi described these, Ram and I glanced at each other and felt we could help with that and put an end to this menace once and for all.

Ah, but then bhabhi read our thoughts and continued: "I obviously was thinking of the best way to help these fine people on our way back from the village. That's when I noticed that we were close to the end of the great Dakshina plateau. And this majestic Godavari river makes its way slowly toward Paudanyapura, after which the land becomes a plain and stretches till the coast. A two-day boat journey on the river from Paudanyapura and you'll reach the vast Vanga Sagara."

I shuffled a bit, showing my restlessness, thinking to myself that we should deal with the Asmaka soldiers first and then worry about Asmaka's trade situation later.

Sita bhabhi seemed oblivious to my thoughts and clearly seemed to enjoy lecturing the room full of students. And Rama was silently enjoying just watching her getting excited about nature. Perhaps Rama was soaking in all this useful knowledge. After all, a future king must know the topology of the land he might have to conquer one day.

Sita: "There is a stretch of canyons and gorges at the end of the plateau where the river traverses in a zigzag manner till it reaches the plains. Note this point, brother dearest," turning toward me suddenly, and then she continued, "Several tall teak trees and big boulders were all strewn all over the river. They must've fallen during the monsoon. Even our makeshift boat was stuck many times. We continued the last part on foot mostly. But what does all this tell you, Anuja?" Again, she turned her peering eyes at me.

I blurted and said, "Good for us. We can use it to make boats and weapons and seek work at Paudanyapura." Everyone glared at me. No sense of humor in them, I suppose.

She answered her own question and said: "It tells me two things. But more on that later."

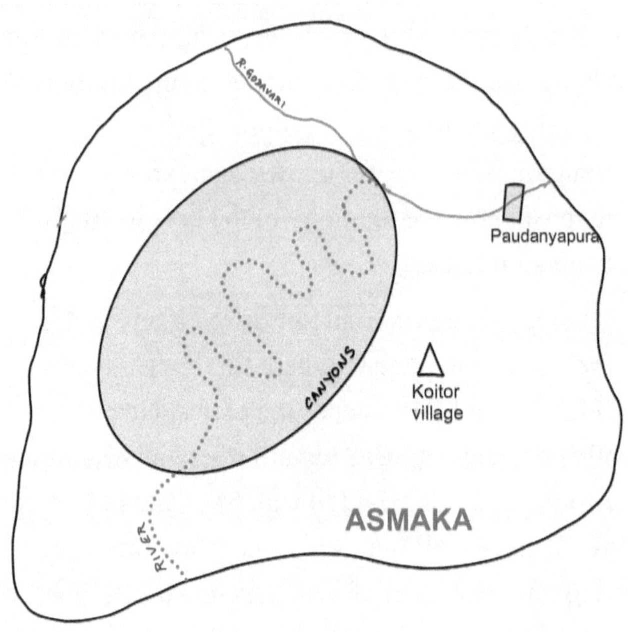

I was getting fidgety. This was a time for action, not imagination. Or so I thought. Everyone else thought otherwise. My eyes were pleading with Rama to intervene, but he too casually smiled and gave an indication to me to be patient. I resigned to a corner.

At this point, Nagamma whispered something to Sara, who then turned to bhabhi and addressed her: "Janakamma, my mother, thank you for going to the village and talking to her clanswomen. She wants to know what they have decided. Would they be surrendering to the King, or would they be fighting them?"

Bhabhi looked at Nagamma kindly and replied: "Neither. Dear lady, your womenfolk are one of the bravest that I have come across. The Koitor women will not surrender that easily. They know life as a slave will be cruel. But they are not gullible either. They know fighting the army means a sure death. They miss a leader like you to advise them and lead them."

Nagamma seemed to have understood what bhabhi said, for she cried inconsolably. We could make out that she felt guilty for abandoning her village. She wanted to get back to them, fight with them, defend the village till the men return. Then, they stand some chance.

Sita: "Don't worry, Nagamma. We will all go there."

Nagamma said something in an anxious tone, which Sara translated as: "What did you tell my people, akka?" Nagamma addressed Sita bhabhi as her sister!

Sita: "The truth, Nagamma. I told them to stay patient till I returned. And prepare. When I was talking to the womenfolk, I observed that they had so much knowledge of the herbs that grew in that part of the forest. They have medicines from various herbs. They have Uppu chekka for knee pain. It's a root that they grind with rice soaked in water. They have Illintha bark, which can be ground with salt and applied over wounds. Even their Bikki bark paste can be applied over the body to get relief from pains. Or Dumpidi, also a crushed bark that is used as a bandage on wounds and cuts. I told them we would need all this for what's ahead."

Rama chuckled at this burst of ayurvedic lecture: "Do you still need Anuja and me?"

Sita retorted and said: "Who do you think will roll the boulders?" And then she walked out. "Roll the boulders?" Rama and I cried in unison.

Chapter 9

One for the Koitor Tribe

By now Luv and Kush sat in front of me, and I could feel their palpitations. They were agog about what would unfold next. They burst out laughing at this repartee.

I took a few more sips of water and continued: "Obviously bhabhi had a plan. And Rama and I were glad to be her sidekicks. But I was just hoping we weren't foolishly trying to be brave. Typically, when we were on the move, we employed the military-style Y-formation while walking. Rama up front and right. Bhabhi would come slightly to his left and back. I was at the rear center. This ensured that we had a better view of our surroundings while avoiding stepping on animal traps or, worse, enemy arrows. Rama took the job of deciding which direction we would take. Bhabhi had the knack of picking up animal tracks and talked about the habitat, the flora and fauna. Her knowledge was such that I used to think she belonged to nature and probably was raised by Mother Earth herself in her childhood! It was rare for royal kinsmen to know so much about nature, let alone royal women. Bhabhi seemed to have gained a deeper insight into the lay of the land. We followed her and Sara as they traced the route back to the canyon, North of the forest. To avoid being spotted, we maintained a distance between each other. After an uneventful journey, we reached the top of the canyon. At that particular spot bhabhi took us, we could see the river snake through narrow gorges. The gorges weren't too deep, so the river did not have too many rapids and thus was still navigable.

Sita stood over the edge of one of the canyons and pointed at the river. She couldn't have picked a more dramatic place to take a geology lesson. I was worried about the loose pebbles and falling rocks, but she seemed one with nature. Rama and I kept a watch to see if there were any soldiers scouting the area. She then conveyed some message to Sara, who quickly started trekking down the gorge.

Sita: "OK, let's camp here and retire for the night. No fire. We don't want to be sitting roasted ducks for the Asmaka scouts. We have a long day ahead tomorrow."

"That's it, brother. I'm taking over command of the operation," I said in a low but forceful voice.

Sita: "Hmm, is that right, brother? Shall I tell you what your plan would be?"

I retorted: "Whatever it is, sister, it would be less talk, more action. And I wouldn't bring women and children to a battlefield."

And I bit my tongue and cursed myself for uncharacteristically uttering the last line. Sita bhabhi and her sisters were themselves examples of some of the finest woman warriors I know. Besides Rama and I were 'children' too when we entered battlefield. And you boys, Luv and Kush, gave Ayodhya soldiers a run for their money few years back. Anyway, I couldn't pull back my words, so I silently looked at Rama.

Meanwhile, Rama was curiously studying the slope of the gorge on the West side, which had a big clearing. Naturally, that must have seen more mudslides.

Sita: "There is a time and place to employ brute force, brother. Now is not it. I know you two heroes can easily take down their entire battalion. That would mean the king would suspect us and possibly risk revealing our identities. More importantly, the little that I have seen of the Koitor tribe, they take immense pride in being independent. They don't like being subjugated nor do they like assistance from outsiders."

Sound logic. I hadn't thought through my approach. I conceded. Again.

Sita continued, having tamed this bull: "Now, my strategy isn't all that complicated. If Asmaka wants slaves to support its thriving river port commerce, let's divert the water. No water, no river. No river, no port! I'll tell you the details of my plan tomorrow."

I sighed. I was too tired to argue and just retreated tactically. Rama? Well, he was enjoying all this. He knew bhabhi better than anyone and he knew her to be a child of nature. Sita bhabhi can show immense patience when necessary and at the same time knows when to take charge of action. Overall, Rama trusted Sita's ability completely. Another sign of a great leader such as your father, Ram. He knew better than to intervene when he saw a talented, amazing leader such as Sita bhabhi being in charge of a mission. His mentality was: 'Let your best person run a mission, provide support, and get out of the way.' Note this down, Luv and Kush. These are valuable lessons for you when one day you will be in charge of leading important assignments. You need to know that taking charge is as important as delegating to a more capable person.

Anyway, back to the story. The next day, the village womenfolk started coming in small batches all through the day. Once they had sufficiently rested, bhabhi called out to them to assemble. She climbed onto a small boulder and addressed them.

Sita: "Ladies, I could not be prouder of you showing courage, patience, and resilience. I know you trust me. I have more faith in you that together we shall give Asmaka a run for their money.

Here's my plan: First, we shall take positions all along the length of the gorge, at the top on the West side. We go in pairs and maintain a distance of one paridesh. Sufficiently far but also near enough to signal each other. If my calculation is right, it will rain tonight. Using pre-agreed sound call-signals, we shall roll the boulders and rocks down the gorge. We use the teak wood logs to act as a lever to wedge the boulders off its surface. Even if someone hears the sound, they might dismiss it as a landslide. Once we have run down enough boulders, we take a hundred paces or about half a krosha[12] in the North westerly direction and repeat. We stop after we have collectively covered five yojanas[12]. Any questions?"

I bet the villagers didn't understand a single word. And I was hoping Rama would object to this plan, but he didn't. Did no one see the folly in this?

---

12   **Krosha, paridesh & yojana** – ancient units of measurement of distances;

     1 paridesh = 125 feet, approximately;

     1 krosha ≈ 3.85 kms, approximately; **4 krosha** = **1 yojana** ≈ 9 miles ≈ 15 kms, approximately;

OK, I understand if the soldiers were waiting down in the gorge, we could roll all kinds of boulders to crush them. But push rocks over a river? Hoping that would divert the majestic Godavari. Madness!

Sita bhabhi turned to me: "Did you catch my drift, brother?"

I mumbled something about a boat loaded with fish and was drifting away. I felt like we were at Guru Vasishta's ashram during our schooling days. I alone used to ask questions back then. My brothers and friends mostly giggled and stayed quiet. Guruji gave me a patient hearing but would silently shake his head. Shatrugna always would come up later and say that my questions were advanced and Guruji didn't want the rest of the students to get confused. That was your Uncle Shatrugna, the ever politically correct one!

Anyway, bhabhi turned back to her obedient audience and continued with her gesture-laden speech: "As I was saying, we roll down the rocks. By doing this, we can control and change the course of the river. By doing that, we can control the flow of water to the port of Paudanyapura. And that will control the size of ships that can berth at the port. By controlling that, we control the fate of Asmaka's commerce. That will teach the King a lesson."

One tap. Then two, then four. And so on... One by one all of us started hitting the logs on the ground.

The rhythmic beats built itself into a tempo that reached a crescendo and turned into a battle cry of:

"Hail leader Janakamma || Glory to Koitor tribe || Victory to our people || Death to anyone in our way."

Just like that. Rhythmic pattern of four lines with each line having eight syllables, sung as an iambic verse, reminiscent of anustubh metre. Poured out from their hearts.

Sita bhabhi took a bow, clearly proud but also embarrassed. I just hoped that the sound should not reach the prying ears of Asmaka soldiers or, if it did, it should have sent a chill down their spines.

The boys were too engrossed in this backstory to react, or blink, or breathe. I smiled, knowing the effect this story would have on them. But my initial smile gave way to pursed lips. The thought of my noble bhabhi brought tears to my eyes.

Finally, Luv broke the silence and asked: "Uncle Lakshman, was the ceremony that some tribal folks were performing back in Ayodhya related to this incident?"

"Yes, my boy. The lady that you saw leading the rituals is that little girl Sara, all grown up. Every year, she accompanies womenfolk from her region to the banks of River Sarayu here. They place small wooden boats with a mud lamp lit on it and let them float on water. Songs, dances, stage puppet shows, and an elaborate feast follow these rituals, for about three days. When you watch these hundreds of boats gently waddling along the river, it resembles fireflies dancing to the tune of their songs. Your father Ram treats them as royal guests and has built shelters for them to stay during this period. The threat from Asmaka had long gone. Nagamma had passed away a few years back. Yet the memories of your mother's leadership and her help had not been forgotten." I stopped after narrating an important but often ignored event from our past.

Just in time too, for my sons Chitrangada and Chandraketu had just joined us in the garden, reminding us that it was time for us to leave Kashi.

Part 4 – A Leader in Action

|| Entharo Maha Anubhava ||

Chapter 10

Lakshmana's Discourse to Chitrangada

"Baba, I really miss my mother. She would guide me well in these situations. She always seemed to know how to prepare my mind. Everything feels different now. I am starting something new in my life without my mother for the first time. That too, without Ketu or you next to me!" Angada replied without taking his eyes off the portrait of his late mother, Urmila.

I came and stood beside him, facing Urmila's portrait and asked him: "Look at your mother's eyes closely. What do they tell you?"

Angada observed the portrait keenly and said: "It almost feels like she is speaking to me with her eyes. Is that even possible?"

"Your mother is always around you. And there are mediums such as this portrait through which she will connect with you. And when she does, all other thoughts fade into oblivion for you. You only hear her voice."

"What do I ask her, father? There are so many thoughts and emotions going through my mind right now. Why, I am even starting to doubt my own ability to handle this new assignment."

"Ah! You don't need to ask her anything, son. You just must focus your mind and convey your feelings. She can understand you and help you navigate through your emotions and help you find answers to your questions."

"But every time I try to focus, I am reminded of the past. Our past, where Ketu and I spent most of our growing years separated from you. Every time I try to control my mind, I have a strong premonition of losing you for good. When I try to think about the future, I am pulled back by self-doubt. I am not sure if I am ready to face the challenges of governing a new place. Can I live up to the lofty standards set by you and my uncles and our ancestors?"

Angada bared his innermost thoughts and deep fear. All these years, I have never been around my sons much. Urmila took care of them and raised them as noble, valiant princes. I turned up and looked at her portrait and realized how much I miss having her at this moment. She would know how to guide him.

I looked at Urmila's portrait and then touched Angada's shoulders and said: "Son, you are worried about things that are not in your control. I am not asking you to forget your past. It is good to have memories of key moments of your life, as that helps keep you grounded. Remembering the past is not akin to inaction. Don't fight that emotion. Let that flow naturally. Your breath and your current actions are the only two things you can control. So, do that. Everything else is speculation. So, avoid that. Planning for the future is good so long as you only think about the impact of your immediate action and not worry about the plan's outcomes. The impact and outcome are two different things, yet they are often misunderstood."

Have you played our *Chaturanga* board game? You know, the game where the moving pieces are shaped like soldiers, ministers, kings, queens, horses or elephants, and the non-movable board represents life? In that game, before you move one piece, you need to anticipate the impact of that move. You may not be able to control the outcome, but you can certainly influence your opponent's action. Similarly, in life, as a leader you will be faced with several choices to make a decision. Pick one that is most logically helping you move ahead in attaining your goals. But when you do take an action, be aware of the reaction. It is especially in such instances when focusing on an image such as this portrait of your mother helps declutter your mind. Do not try to live up to the standards of our ancestors. Rather, focus on just this one mission for now. Your time will come when you will have opportunities to demonstrate your worth. With the pedigree of your lineage, the training you have received, and the strength of your character, I am confident that you will set out to accomplish anything you desire."

"Thank you, father. Do you know something else? I admire how you, Uncle Ram, and Aunt Sita overcame adversities. Even now, with his attention turned toward a looming threat from the Chyavanas, how did he think of planning for the future? I often wonder how Uncle Ram not only stayed strong but also found a way to motivate others around him. Take the instance when Aunt Sita was kidnapped: anyone in his position would have done something rash in their anger. However, not only did Uncle Ram control his grief, but he was also able to rally an entire army, belonging to a different kingdom, to march to Lanka. As I reflect on the stories that you have been sharing over the past few days, I am in awe of how strong Uncle Ram must have been to do something that no one has ever done. I often ask myself, 'How does one venture to undertake a mission when there are no precedents to that and dare to take out-of-box approach?' For instance, build a bridge to

Lanka and take an entire army to cross. I don't know if I can think something like that. Maybe it is the fear of failure that is bothering me now, especially since I am about to embark on a journey that not many have done before. Perhaps if you could share some episodes of Uncle Ram and how he rescued Aunt Sita, that would motivate me and remove my fears."

Hmm, this might take more time than I thought! I just came to wish Angada well and see him off to Kalinga before Ketu and I head out to Malwa. Instead, I find my son hesitating to take that important first step forward. Many great kings and warriors have faced this demon in their mind that they have to vanquish before they act. Hesitation is the strongest of all enemies. I felt that if perhaps I share some anecdotes from the episode of Rama's greatest act, that may help Angada overcome his self-doubt.

So, I replied: "Indeed, son. Let me narrate some of the events you may not know, just as they unfolded during the last phase of our vanavasa. You will understand Rama's vision, his thought process, and his razor-sharp focus."

Chapter 11

Rama and Sugreeva Exchange Favors

Angada, at the time period you indicated, we were in this territory called Kishkinda, which as you know now is the land between Krishna and Pampa rivers. It is now ruled by your namesake, King Angada, who is the son of the great warrior Vali.

Let me take you back to the time Rama and I spent in Kishkinda. We were in King Sugreeva's palace. One day, Sugreeva and I were playing a board game, with Rama assisting the King.

Rama: "If you move your tiger to that square on the right plank, Lakshmana will move his goat one square back and two squares left. Then the only possible move you have is for that tiger to move further right, which would then create an opening and he can take his goats to safety," said Rama, as he was coaching *Kishkinda King Sugreeva* on the moves on the board game of 'Goats and Tigers' or as they call it in those parts: *Aadu-Puli-Aattam*.

At that time, it had been nearly four months since Sita bhabhi had been kidnapped by the Lanka King Ravana. And it was our final year of our vanavasa. The first few days after she was kidnapped were exhausting physically and mentally for us. More for Rama, naturally. We trekked in a Southern direction till one day we came across the noble, aging but dying chief of the vulture clan – Jatayu. He was on his deathbed and as we went near him, we could make out a few words before he took his last breath. Just then Sampati – Jatayu's brother – rushed over, saw his brother lying dead and wept. We waited a few moments for him to calm down before we introduced ourselves and gave our condolences to Sampati. When he learned of our tragedy, along with his information of a fight that Jatayu was having single-handedly and based on a few words of Jatayu that we relayed back, it appeared as if the noble Jatayu got injured in a fight with Ravana. Sampati felt that Jatayu must have tried to rescue princess Sita from Ravana but was unsuccessful. And he guessed that the most likely place for Ravana to hold Sita bhabhi as a hostage would be in Lanka. Now you must realize that all of us in Aryavarta have heard of Ravana and Lanka. But we had no idea how to get there nor how difficult it could be to reach there.

Even now when I think about it, I cannot believe how Sita bhabhi vanished as if she was carried by the wind. That wily old fox Mareecha, who was the uncle of Ravana, set a diversion for Rama and me. That left bhabhi alone in our hut for a few hours. In that interval, Ravana and his band of soldiers, nay thieves, kidnapped bhabhi. Meanwhile, we gave chase to Mareecha and killed him. As we returned to our hut, we found it to be empty. We searched around looking for Sita bhabhi but could not find her. The place looked like there was some scuffle. Our sparse belongings were either scattered on the floor or broken. We panicked and looked for clues everywhere. Besides some broken bangles and small trinkets inside a torn piece of cloth, we found nothing else. Bhabhi must have dropped them even as she must've been battling Ravana. That's Sita bhabhi. Always thinking smartly about the next move. Unfortunately, though, there weren't enough clues for us to mount a rescue. We followed the trail of where Ravana must have gone, using clues such as broken twigs, disturbed plants, bird screeches, etc. till we met the dying Jatayu and his brother Sampati. It was Sampati that suggested we seek Kishkinda King Vali's assistance.

In fact, as I think about it, it happened the other way round. As we were proceeding further down South toward Kishkinda's capital, we came across Sugreeva's trusted and able man Friday, Hanuman. He came with a rather cryptic message from prince Sugreeva. The note read:

"Meet me on the banks of River Pampa at sunset. My man will guide you to the spot. I have some the information you need to aid in the search for your wife. You shall not regret it." I was circumspect. What if this was yet another trap by Ravana? And this time, what if it was us that could be captured?

However, by then our hopes of finding Sita bhabhi were dwindling and we didn't have much choice. So, we went with Sugreeva's aide. Hanuman was a fine young man. Tall, wiry, and rugged, he was at least ten years younger to me. Like most people from the Vanara clan, he had a heavy dose of facial hair and was hirsute in general. Even as we followed him, my mind was thinking about Rama's first words when we came to this land. Both of us were in great anguish having lost Sita bhabhi. Rama was lamenting to me and I still cannot forget his words. He cried: 'Oh! Lakshmana, magnificent is Pampa with its cat's-eye gem-like waters, and she with her fully blossomed lotuses beaming forth, along with many trees around her. Oh! If only Sita was here to enjoy its beauty.'"

I paused here and wiped some of my tears. Narrating these rarely spoken anecdotes gave me goosebumps. I wasn't the only one. Even Angada's eyes had welled with tears.

I continued narrating: "Soon, we reached a small grove by the River Pampa whence Sugreeva, the estranged prince of Kishkinda, jumped down from a tree. Sugreeva was furtive. He had as much reason not to trust us as we did him. Anyway, as things go, we soon bonded over a common cause of losing something dear and valuable to us. Sugreeva explained how he was hiding in his own kingdom to avoid being captured by his brother Vali – the present King of Kishkinda. Apparently, Vali was coming off a recent battle where he was victorious in defeating some of his perennial enemies. So, by way of celebration, Vali had lately been spending less time at the royal court and instead was more interested in drinking and dancing with the nymphs. He was gradually losing the support of his friends and allies. He had this network of spies who were feeding him lies about Sugreeva joining hands with traitors. Vali suspected Sugreeva and his coterie of plotting to kill him and take over the throne. So, he started assassinating all those he perceived as a threat. Sugreeva somehow escaped with a few of his trusted friends such as Hanuman, Jambavan, Nala, Nila, and a few others. One day, from their hideout up at the Anjanadri hills, named after Hanuman's mother and late princess Anjana, they spotted a small troop of soldiers sailing down River Pampa. Upon closer observation, they deduced that it was Ravana, King of Lanka along with a few soldiers. With them was a prisoner – a lady – whose hands and legs were tied up. Initially, Sugreeva thought that Ravana was on his way to meet Vali, carrying a prisoner. This was a natural assumption, for Vali and Ravana knew each other for a long time. In fact, they both went to the same Gurukul for a few years in their younger days. However, they weren't on the best of terms of late. So then, what was Ravana doing in these parts? Why have they taken a prisoner, that too a woman, who did not look like she was from the Vanara clan? She was either some nobility or a merchant's daughter. But basically, not someone important enough to be held hostage for a ransom. Meanwhile, Sugreeva's spies had gathered some intel on this. They found a bracelet and lapis lazuli stone-studded earrings on the other side of the river. And they also learned that King Vali was unaware of Ravana's presence here. Besides, it appeared from atop the Anjanadri hills that Ravana seemed to be sailing in a hurry down the river. They surmised that, perhaps, he was sailing to the East Coast and then onwards toward Lanka in the South.

Rama and I were completely engrossed in this report. It still did not give us what we were looking for, but at least we gathered some new information.

More importantly, we knew Sita bhabhi was alive. But we also had several questions. What was Ravana doing this far North? Was this Vali fellow somehow involved? What was their game? Why did Ravana have to kidnap bhabhi? Or did he not know he was capturing Sita bhabhi and maybe he mistook her to be some young lady that happened to be in that forest area at the same time? All in all, his motives were unclear. His actions were even more peculiar. We learned from Sugreeva that the coquette Surpanaka whom we encountered back in our hut and caused injury, was Ravana's sister. Well, I can't be blamed. All I did was push her away when she tried to hug me in our hut. She hit a wall and got a bloodied nose. It was a minor cut. She ran away and I thought that was that. How could I know that she was Ravana's sister? Or that she would have spun a story so convincing for Ravana to come all the way over here to kidnap Sita bhabhi? And that too in just a matter of a few days? Anyway, all that is past. We had heard of the legendary battle that Ravana has had with the Aryavarta kingdoms and how he was a threat to the stability and economy of Aryavarta. For someone like that to simply kidnap a harmless lady is beneath his dignity and status. Not only that, but to launch an audacious kidnapping in a foreign kingdom is nothing short of espionage of the highest order. What if he had a bigger and more sinister design in his mind?

If Kishkinda King Vali gets to hear about this, would he not declare war on Lanka? And in that melee, what happens to the safety of Sita bhabhi? More questions than we had answers for.

Weeks passed since Rama agreed to help Sugreeva vanquish Vali and get him the throne of Kishkinda. The cloak which we were wearing had come off the moment Ravana kidnapped Sita bhabhi. No more being incognito. Rama decided he would bring Sita back to safety. Our fourteen years were just a few months away. No point in hiding in the woods. Over the next month, a lot had happened. Rama killed Vali in a duel, as per the agreement Rama had with Sugreeva, and secured the throne of Kishkinda for Sugreeva. Not even Vali's closest allies shed tears. Vali was becoming very unpopular. His own son, Angada, had sided with his uncle Sugreeva.

Initially, Sugreeva spent all his energy to gain more political control and general acceptance from his people on his kingship. He had requested our help in organizing and training his army. He wanted to learn battle strategies and statecraft. He wanted to merge Kishkinda with the broader Aryavarta domain.

At first, I was a bit surprised by Rama's decision to ally with Sugreeva, as Rama had always believed in upholding Dharmic values, either as crown prince, or as a brother, or as a husband. What then motivated him to help unseat King Vali? Did he believe Vali was undeserving of the throne he was sitting on? Or did he think Vali secretly abetted Ravana's mercenaries and was indirectly involved in the kidnapping of Sita bhabhi? Or did he think Sugreeva would make a better king than Vali, whom he had not met? We only knew of Vali's excesses from Sugreeva. For all we knew, that could be an exaggeration. When bards of future generations write about this, they may argue whether Rama's actions were right or not. Let them. That's what bards do. Anyway, I supported this move as sometimes the greater good trumps immediate exigencies. Vali was developing hegemonistic traits. He had usurped Sugreeva's own wife. He had ill-treated Angada. He basically espoused all virtues that a King ought not to do. I suppose that is enough reason for Rama, from a moral standpoint, to vanquish him.

After becoming the king, Sugreeva consulted us regularly. But he was mindful of the fact that Rama and I were in exile and thus we couldn't live in his palace quarters, nor could he get us to invoke assistance from Ayodhya formally. In our individual capacities, we did our best to help train his army using traditional as well as innovative approaches. For instance, Rama used the Aadu-Puli-Aattam game, which seemed to have been played around in these parts for centuries, to teach war games, moves and counter moves. Notwithstanding all this, it had been raining for over three months without a break. Rama and I were whiling away our time in our simple makeshift shelter in the outskirts of the capital city.

That was the day, as yet another round of this board game ended, when Rama snapped. Even as we were playing the game, King Sugreeva stretched his neck and lazily went after yet another cup of arrack, a local fermented alcohol. Suddenly, Rama sat upright, stared down and his muscles tightened. I knew the telltale signs when Rama got angry. He would purse his lips tight, would not blink his eyes and would generally look down at the floor. He looked up and said: "King Sugreeva. It is time for us to leave. My brother and I are grateful for your hospitality and your offer to help us find my wife Sita. You are now busy handling your administrative responsibilities, consolidating political power and focusing on rebuilding Kishkinda. I don't want to trouble you further. As soon as the rain stops, we shall proceed."

Just a month prior to that, Sugreeva had dispatched his elite spashs, or spies, across various corners. I remember that Sugreeva had made a great speech out of what could've just been an order. His words were flowery, but the instruction detailed, clearly indicating the geographical awareness and reach that this kingdom had. His instructions to his spies were in the form of a speech that I still remember: 'You shall first behold the Vindhya ranges, possessing a hundred peaks covered with trees and shrubs of every kind, and the enchanting river, Narmada, frequented by mighty serpents, and the wide and charming stream, Godavari, with its dark reeds, and the captivating Krishnaveni; the regions of Mekhalas and Utkala and the city of Dasharna also; Abravanti and Avanti, Vidarbhas and Nishtikas and the charming Mahishakas. You will see too, the Matsyas, Kalingas and Kaushikas, where you should search for the princess and the Dandaka Forest with its mountains, rivers and caverns and the Godavari, also examine the districts of *Andhras, Paundras, Cholas, Pandyas and Keralas.*' Then return to the Ayomukha Mountain, rich in ore, with its marvelous peaks and flowering woodlands; that mountain, possessing lovely forests of sandalwood, should be carefully searched by you.' As I was saying, once you get to know him, you get used to his theatrics.

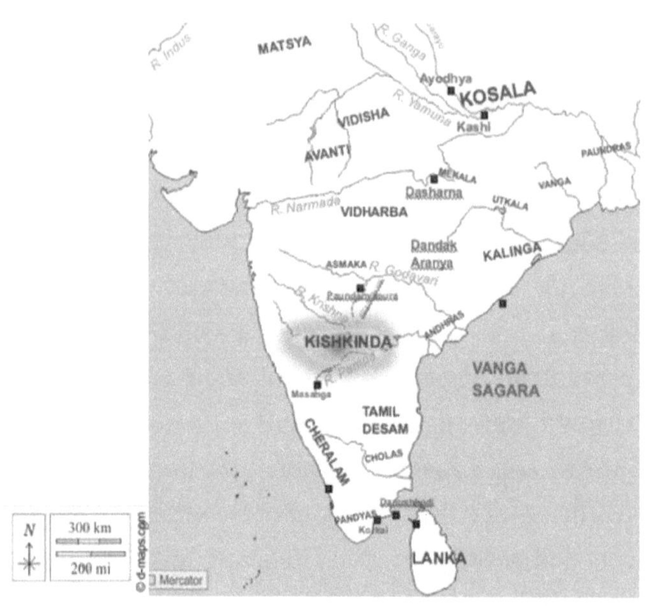

However, due to the monsoons, the spies were delayed in returning. Eventually, the ones from the West, East and North returned but had no further news of bhabhi or Ravana. That left Hanuman, who was dispatched South, as the only one yet to return.

Anyway, after Rama's outburst that day, Sugreeva pulled himself up, waved off the cup, and splashed some water on his face. He took on a formal tone as that of a king and said: "Prince Rama! I am deeply sorry to have put you in this position." And in a loud voice, he continued, "Kishkinda is honored to have hosted you and your brother. And your pain is our pain. Your problem is our problem. Rest assured. I have dispatched my most trusted ally and friend Hanuman to Lanka. He never fails. If there is anyone that can overcome any challenge, it is he."

Rama interjected rather uncharacteristically and said "Dear friend and King Sugreeva. We are honored to have been your allies. But as you can imagine, any delay puts my wife in greater danger. There is no telling what Ravana is capable of. While thus far we have not heard a word from Lanka, it is only a matter of time. By now Ravana must have known about Vali's death. He might suspect your hand in this too. He might sense an opportunity to foment trouble by sending an emissary here. He could twist the kidnapping event to his advantage and claim that his sister Surpanaka and uncle Mareecha were harmed and killed in your kingdom and thus would place ransom demands on you. Imagine if they found out that we were harbored by you here. Thus, it won't be appropriate for us to stay any longer."

Sugreeva was taken aback. If he was tipsy earlier, he was sober by now. He went into deep thought. He understood the full implications of hosting Rama and Lakshmana longer than necessary. But he also weighed the advantages of having them as trusted advisers and good friends. He replied: "My friend. I now understand your position much better. But I too have some tricks up my sleeve. Hear me out." Before proceeding to say anything further, he asked his attendants and guards to vacate his chambers. Clearly, he was taking precautions to ensure there were no Ravana's spies among his inner staff. Smart. Perhaps a bit too sober.

He continued: "The monsoons are still in full flow and any emissary would have to first sail up the coast of *Keezh-Karai-Mandalam*, or as you Aryavartans call it, the East Coromandel Coast. Unlike a spy, the emissary must take a royal Lankan navy tugboat with all the paraphernalia of a royal embassy. That makes them a bit slower to reach here and more obvious. Our people are keeping a watch over there and I have not heard from any of them yet. It might mean that Ravana is waiting for the coast to clear, so to speak. Not only that, but my men have also traced back the training camp of Mareecha and found that he and a few others were encamped in the outskirts of Dandaka Forest, close to Mount Ayomukha. He seems to have been here for several years but what their activities were, we know not. Anyway, we have recovered a few artifacts that belong to him and the Lankan royals. Clearly, this is a violation and infringement of our territory. Thus, if any emissary comes from Lanka, I know how to turn the tables on them and instead demand that Lanka pay for the damages, along with the repatriation of princess Sita. If all else fails, and if war is the only last option left, then my entire army is at your disposal, and I will personally lead it."

That was indeed a high-spirited speech! But I must admit, his plan was sound and logical. Rama too seemed clearly impressed with Sugreeva. He slowly relented his anger and spoke: "My friend. Please forgive me if I have spoken in a harsh tone. Surely you can understand my eagerness to repatriate Sita as soon and as safely as possible. However, as you said, we shall wait to hear back from Hanuman or for the rains to end, whichever is sooner. After that, we shall decide on the next course of action. Till then, we shall continue with the training for your army. Lakshmana will work with Jambavan to organize the battalions under each regiment and the regiments under a division, which serves a specific purpose. I will work with Nala to discuss logistics. Please convene your war Council in two weeks. No matter where Ravana has kept Sita captive, we will march there. But before that, let us hope Hanuman reaches us with some news."

Great! It looked like even my brother seemed to have joined this speech contest.

Chapter 12

Preparation for the March

———◆◆———

The next few days saw a series of meetings, activity and a general hustle and bustle. The normally quiet Kishkinda capital at this time of the year during rains came alive. The war Council had been assembled. Messengers were sent forth to various corners of the kingdom to inform local chieftains to send their troops. Unlike most of Aryavarta, the Dravida desa was more decentralized. Although the King held a standing army in his capital, he relied upon local chieftains to supply their regular and reserve forces. This was a win-win for both. Wars can be lucrative for the chieftains. They can decide best on their military size. Besides, the King need not have so many personnel on active duty thereby reducing the cost. The cities down South were also smaller compared to their Northern counterparts. The only disadvantage Kishkinda had was that their army never had to travel very far to fight battles. They needed to be prepared to go to Lanka should we find that Sita bhabhi was held captive there. Kishkinda army was perfectly suited for guerilla missions, mountain warfare and surgical strikes. Throw in ground battle, laying siege for an extended period or naval battles, then you are looking at a disaster when faced with such a type of war.

While it wasn't possible for Rama and me to train or redesign their entire army to suit all these styles, we needed to prepare them with a minimum credible deterrence. Rama suggested that we deploy more divisions on defense and then fewer offensive units to carry out strikes. We were there not to fight Ravana's entire army but to mount a rescue mission. Or so we thought. Who knows what surprise we have in store. The strength of Ravana's army carries a combination of well-fed myths and past glory. It had been decades since his army had ventured out of Lanka. Their military composition had changed as well. The word is when Ravana overthrew his half-brother Visravana from Lanka's throne, most of the naval strength depleted. Apparently, he was a master naval strategist. Ravana built lavish palaces in the center of Lanka's Malaya Rata province. These were high mountains surrounded by dense forest. Luckily for us, Kishkinda's Vanara army is adept at fighting battles in such terrains. But the mother of all our challenges is still going to be the great crossing! How do we get to Lanka without big ships, which Kishkinda does not have, or nearest point, of which our knowledge was poor? Sugreeva was not in the greatest of terms with coastal warlords, so we might have to cross unsafe territory.

Maybe a decentralized economy and administration wasn't all that perfect. Perhaps I am being selfish as my mission was to help Rama rescue Sita bhabhi and we could use all kinds of allies in the world to achieve that. That said, a decentralized economy works well if done right. I did notice the strong cultural links each of the kingdoms shared. The primary bond among the Southern territories is their affinity toward their own language – the Dravida bhasha. Most people believe that this language is older than what we speak up in Aryavarta. Someone coined the term Deva bhasha for the language we speak up North, to distinguish from Dravida bhasha that is spoken down South. I have heard Guru Vishwamitra and Guru Agastya mention that we all had common ancestors that lived along the legendary River Saraswati. If that was indeed true, then great indeed is the broader Bharata Desa.

It has been ten days since that meeting with Sugreeva. Rains continued to pour down, albeit with lesser intensity and frequency. The dark clouds have given way to, well, less dark clouds. There was more wind than rain. Rama was in his morning prayers at a temple for Muruga, as Lord Subrahmanya was known in these parts. Looking at him pray reminded me of the time when Sage Vishwamitra narrated to Rama and me the story and deeds of Lord Muruga. Among the many stories that the Sage told us, the tale of Lord Skanda or Muruga filled us with renewed vigor before we encountered Yakshi Tataka. Similarly, even today, we need the Lord's blessings to lift us from this grave situation that we were facing.

Our hut was very close to this temple, located in a hamlet called *Onake Kindi*, at the foothills of Mount Ayomukha. A dolmen rather than a hut, in fact. Dolmens were these giant slabs of rocks set in such a way that there were at least four or six tall standing pillars spaced about two *dhanush* units apart, arranged in a closed loop, and giant boulder pieces placed across these pillars like a roof. We were told that these were laid by ancestors of the Vanars, usually a burial site of an important person, perhaps a clan chief or priest. Some of these were used by miners. Ours was an abandoned place. There was residue of some blackish mud. The miners must have been attempting to smelt the ore to extract new minerals that they were hoping to find.

I took a pause here from my narration for two reasons. One was to see if Angada had any questions. But the other main reason is, as I was reminiscing about this story, something struck me. And that is, back then when Rama and I were staying in that hamlet Onake Kindi, I had noticed that there were also a few stone temples in honor of the Goddess in the form of Bhadra Kali. And as I think about it, I recall that usually the mainstream Vanara people typically worship Lord Muruga. However, the native tribes frequented goddess Kali temples. To their credit, the Kishkinda royals allowed both sects to live their respective ways of life. Nevertheless, I need to verify some of these facts with Hanuman when I meet him next.

Meanwhile, I continued with my narration: "Angada, one common thing we noticed in Kishkinda was that their temples were made of stones quarried from nearby hills. Whereas we Aryavartans typically build our temples near a river or a stream. Now, when I say stones, I mean rocks. Kishkinda, especially near the great River Pampa, has an endless array of smooth rocks and boulders strewn all over the place. Big rocks, medium rocks, smooth rounded rocks. Rocks of all shapes and sizes. This made it easier to construct buildings or anicuts by simply rolling these boulders. The Kishkinda Engineers had an ingenious way of making simple locks carved in the boulders with which they could join two rocks. Since Rama would not stay in the capital nor would he want any sign of luxury, we stayed at one such place. But for Rama and me, the place we were staying was quite spacious and comfortable. Additionally, the dolmens were always built on high ground, giving us a vantage point to watch for any predators or bandits or enemies."

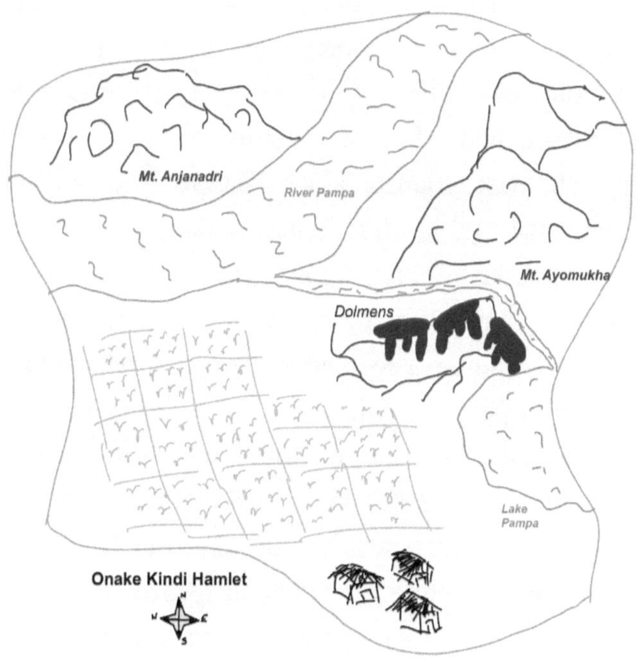

As Rama was praying, I was getting ready to head to the cantonment. Rama and I were going to review the army supplies. Carrying, managing, and replenishing supplies, especially in a potential long march to unfamiliar land, is tricky. You carry too much of it, it slows down the march. You carry too little, and should you then find yourself in unfamiliar terrain, you risk starvation. It is important to carry dried meat, dried fruit and nuts, and sufficient medicinal herbs. As for pots, well, we may well end up at the coast where there are coconut trees, and the shells act as good storage and cooking vessels. Then we must worry about tools, weapons, tents, boats, ropes. That was Nila's department. Nila was Nala's twin. Like me and Shatrughna. Hmmm, Shatrughna. I really miss him. His wise counsel always helped me untangle complicated and vexing issues, and he always read my mind. Like him, this Nila can read Nala's thoughts even without words being exchanged. And he was very organized. Sugreeva seemed to have very talented and resourceful people in his Inner Council. For instance, Nila had calculated the maximum weight of supplies each Vanara soldier should carry. He knows his brother Nala, the Engineer, would care about all such finer details. In fact, this metric would prove to be very vital, as we would later find out. Speaking of details, one aspect about all this is a mystery to me. How and from where did Ravana and his band enter and exit Kishkinda so quickly and stealthily? Do they have a spy network that helped them with logistics? Or did they have special modes of transport that we are not aware of? If so, we may be fighting a professional enemy unit that is far superior with tactical advantages. I really hoped Hanuman comes back with vital intelligence.

Beyond brute power and fighting ability, it is intelligence data that always tilts the balance of any war. It is what we in Aryavarta are trained by our teachers Vasishta and Vishwamitra to pay attention to.

Rama has this extraordinary ability to switch his attention from one aspect to another seamlessly. One moment he would be with me talking about his vision for Ayodhya and how to rule and administer the Aryavarta republics. Another moment he would be with Sita bhabhi appreciating nature, having philosophical conversations about life and our purpose on Earth. A rather one-sided conversation, really. Sita bhabhi was a great debater, and you don't want to counter her with facts. Another time, Rama would be this dutiful shishya amidst Rishis, being proper with the protocols, language, and questions. Or when we go out hunting, he would put on his game face, maintain stoic silence, maintain calmness and patience however long it takes, and be precise with his arrows. One arrow, usually.

Chapter 13

Hanuman Brings News about Sita

It was early morning. Rama and I were just getting ready to go to the river temple for our morning prayers and exercise when a messenger barged in. We didn't hear him come up and instinctively took our knives. But better sense prevailed. He must've run from the palace and up the hillock to reach our dolmen. He wanted to say something for he was panting for breath. Rama went up to him, patted him on the shoulder, and offered some water. He slowly stood upright and was able to speak a little: "Respec… Sir…. Come… urgen…. Lord Hanu…. Lord…. Han…u... Hanuman. Come. Hall….."

Rama and I looked at each other, partly in anticipation of some development, and partly worried if there was any grave word about Sita bhabhi. Rama looked at the soldier and asked: "My dear man. Take a breath. Who are you? Are you asking us to come somewhere now? Where? And did something happen to Hanuman?"

The soldier said, a little better: "Sir… no time to… will be flogged…. I take you now…. Lord Hanuman is waiting for you. King is waiting…."

That was enough for us. We quickly poured water on our faces, took our bows, and followed the soldier as he started sprinting back toward the palace.

Even as we were going, I could see the morning dawn slowly starting to come out of its hiding among the clouds. It must have rained all night. But right now, there was only a slight drizzle, making the air cool. We were able to proceed quickly to Pampa, from there a short boat ride, and then again, a quick sprint toward the fort entrance.

The palace itself was atop a hill, and the path leading to it was narrow and lined with shops that sold everything from everywhere. As the grand assembly was in session, there were more crowds than usual. The usual entourage of people that accompany chieftains from other places of the kingdom spent time roaming the streets, enjoying the local food, sweets and drink, or shopping. Travelers loved the local street delicacies of millet balls stuffed with jaggery and coconut, downed with a strong fermented drink that had various ingredients. As Kishkinda was situated at an important trade route where the Dakshina-pada or the Southern Highway crossed Pampa, one could find merchants from various parts of Bharata Desa and even from far-off places such as Lanka, Sumeria, or Kemet – the land of the Nile and Pyramids. As this was toward the end of the monsoon, fresh goods from Nabatean-Arab ports had landed on the port town of Sopara, situated on the West coast of the Konkan region. From there, goods were transported on smaller boats that sailed up the Bhima river, onto the Krishna river, and then to the River Pampa. These merchants traded their goods and spent time for a few months before sailing back during the winter season. Kishkinda profited from this through the tax they collected from boats crossing their land on to Kalinga and Vanga desa. The Vanars themselves weren't particularly good at trade, but the land hosted several merchant guilds and offered ship repair and other trade support services. The people also had a flair for languages, so several locals operated as guides to the visiting merchants. Some even stayed in their employment full-time.

As Rama and I reached the gates, we showed the royal insignia to the guards who not only allowed us entry but also accompanied us to the Assembly Hall using a shorter route. The maha-sabha hall was situated on the North side of the palace. Typically, the Council was convened in the evening. The assembly room itself was a long hall aligned in the East-West direction with the King's throne placed at the East end and the Council members' chairs, which were like large couches, placed on either side lengthwise. At the West end was a big window through which the sun rays fell on the throne during sunset. This was considered auspicious as the Vanara royals considered themselves as scions of the Suryavanshis.

All these thoughts went in a blur. I was worried more about meeting Hanuman. What shape was he in? Was he injured, unconscious, or did he return successfully back carrying some useful information about bhabhi?

When we reached there, we saw over two dozen chieftains talking among each other in smaller groups. Perhaps they were catching up after a long time. I saw Hanuman alone in the far end, pacing the corner by himself. Thank God, he was in one piece.

Just then the sentries started announcing the name, title, and lineage of the Vanara clan. But they were cut short when King Sugreeva rushed in. He paused, saw the hall quickly, spotted Hanuman, went up to him, and embraced him warmly. Their friendship was genuine, and the respect that each had for the other was also genuine. He whispered something in Hanuman's ears, who then came in our direction. Meanwhile, Rama was quiet through this whole journey from our hut. But I could hear his mind voice. He was tense, uptight with pursed lips, and blinked sparingly. As Hanuman came near us, he paused, gave his customary salute to Rama, and bowed. He didn't say a word, but he had a twinkle in his eyes and curled lips. His sense of humor seemed to be back, and the playfulness returned to his smile. I was just glad to see him in one piece.

Rama reached and held Hanuman's forearms, patted him, and just said: "My friend. How are you? I am so happy to see you."

Hanuman: "vāmadēvāya namō – Glory be to Shiva! Lord Rama, blessed indeed are these eyes that saw Lady Sita in good health, albeit a prisoner and waiting for you to defeat Ravana."

Bravo! He doesn't beat around the bush. As straight to the point as Rama's arrows. Clearly conveyed the most important news that Rama has been waiting for and yet conveyed every aspect he wanted to hear. Okay, so we know Ravana has not harmed bhabhi. And she seemed to be in good spirits. The choice of words is exactly what bhabhi would have said.

Rama: "Where is Sita and do tell what you saw?"

Hanuman: "Shall I tell it all to the Council?" Rama nodded. This Hanuman is not just brave but also diplomatic. Wise for his age. Sugreeva has chosen well.

Sugreeva clapped twice. All the Council leaders took their assigned seats. Rama sat next to the King, and I stood behind Rama. Hanuman stood facing King Sugreeva.

Sugreeva then addressed the assembly: "Dear Council members, clan leaders, and respected elders. I welcome you to Kishkinda. Our dear nation is facing danger from the dreaded enemy – Lanka King Ravana. You can understand the urgency and importance of convening this esteemed assembly."

He paused for a bit, surveyed the hall, and keenly watched for any reaction from the members. Silence. One elder stood up and posited: "King Sugreeva. In my six decades of long experience, I have stood by your father Surya and served Kishkinda. I know Ravana well. He may have Aryavarta roots, but he envisions himself as the champion of Dravida tradition. He has made Lanka a trade destination from all sorts of lands. He has stabilized Lanka's politics and economy and pulled them out of the chaos that they were during the times of Visravana. Pray tell us what reason you must believe that we are in danger from him."

Sugreeva continued: "Respected elder Bujanga. You honor me with your continued support, just as you did to my father. You may know of Ravana. But you may not be aware that he is not himself these past few years. Ever since my rogue of a brother Vali took to drinking and paid little attention to the administration, Ravana sensed an opening to invade us. He has always fancied gaining this great land of ours, eyeing our strategic inland trade location and to mount his future expedition of wars with our Northern neighbors. That is why he has allied with Andhras and Pandyas and funded their projects. Why? So that he can count on their support as and when he invades us. Our spies also uncovered a hideout where his uncle Mareecha and a few others were camped, and we believe that place was their terror cell. Thus, his sister deliberately instigated a skirmish with our friends Lord Rama and Lord Lakshmana but got injured in the process. Ravana then used this minor issue to stealthily smuggle himself in, kidnap respected Lady Sita, and is now holding her hostage in Lanka. That coward sent an emissary a few days back to demand ransom. Ravana's all-familiar tactics involve first threat, then coercion, then guerilla attacks and finally full-scale battle. It is a war of attrition that he has perfected over the years. After a prolonged internal struggle, he dethroned his nitwitted half-brother Visravana. But I suspect that was just an elaborate show. I am sure Visravana has been deployed with his naval fleet and money to foment trouble in some foreign land."

At this stage, another clan chief rose up and spoke: "Respected King. I thank you for your vision and for protecting our land and our economy from the wiles of that wicked Ravana. I agree that Ravana must be stopped in his tracks so that he does not dare to come near us. However, I am concerned whether we are ready to face an enemy as powerful as he is. We are just coming off a civil war ourselves and have just managed to defeat the traitors that sided with Vali. We are barely rebuilding our army and our economy. Are we ready for another war that is far too large in scale? Besides, we don't have sufficient reason to believe that Lady Sita is in Lanka. We went with the words of chief Sampati, but even he was not fully sure of that. Lastly, how do we go all-in to this war against Lanka, in Lanka, for a cause that is not even ours?"

Wah! First sign of opposition. Although I fully understand where these selfish chiefs are coming from. They must protect their turf. And sure, they don't know if they would return alive from Lanka. King Sugreeva must have full backing before he can commit to sending his troops. But I was getting mad at this endless argument and debate. And I suspect I am not the only one. The King himself was fidgeting and getting annoyed. However, Rama was staring at the floor. I know his mind. He must be thinking that they should allow Hanuman to speak, so we could hear from him a firsthand account of the situation. Rama and I were determined to go to Lanka, even if that meant going alone.

King Sugreeva flared up and said: "Dattagama! Watch your words. Are you questioning our great Vanara army's valor and honor? Do you think we would let our friends suffer alone? Have you forgotten the help Lord Rama gave in defeating Vali? Ravana is at best as powerful as Vali, if not more. With our entire army, under the able guidance of Lord Rama, we can cross rivers, oceans and mountains if it means we need to rescue Lady Sita. In any case, surely you know Ravana. He would use any excuse to attack us. I bet he is utilizing this time to plan an attack on us."

Sugreeva continued: "Let us hear from our friend Hanuman. He has just returned from Lanka. He has met Lady Sita. He has gathered all the intelligence we need."

That shut that crackpot clan chief Dattagama up. There was hush and murmur. This is news to most of the members in the hall. Hanuman was a popular adviser and trusted aide to King Sugreeva. And he had proven himself in strength and intelligence over the years. Thus, when he rose to speak, the whole hall listened.

Hanuman: "Respected King, respected elders, respected clan chiefs, respected Lords Rama and Lakshmana. I bow before you for trusting me with the responsibility to spy on Lanka. With your blessings, I was able to do that. I bring back with me location, layout, and other details. With your permission, I would like to submit them to this esteemed assembly."

Always polite, maybe a tad too polite. I am not sure if this assembly is truly worthy of all the permission and blessing. It is no wonder Hanuman has been able to work with everyone.

King Sugreeva looked to Rama and said: "Lord Rama. Do we have your permission for Hanuman to share details of Lady Sita's state of captivity, location, and other necessary details?"

Rama: "Thank you, King Sugreeva, and the respected assembly members. I request Hanuman to spare no details."

Chapter 14

Ram Setu

Three weeks after the grand assembly session, we started marching. Hanuman was simply brilliant. He had somehow figured out where Sita bhabhi was held captive. He snuck in, met and spoke to her. My proud dear bhabhi, as suspected, refused to come back with him. She wanted Rama to punish Ravana and then come take her. Hanuman got captured, was summoned to the court of Ravana and got arrested. Somehow, he escaped from the dungeons. But wait. Not before he set the entire prison on fire along with several adjacent buildings where the army supplies and weapons were stored. Short of destroying the entire Lankan army, he has done everything. May Lord Rudra bless this young irrepressible Braveheart.

Hanuman provided vital intelligence around the route, campgrounds, supplies, villages, and army strength. Rama reviewed the entire war manual with Sugreeva. Lanka clearly had a numerical advantage, but their army was not in fighting mode compared to that of the Vanara army. Besides, the recent economic success of Lanka had made them more docile. The word was they were struggling to recruit men for the army and were mulling conscription. The younger men prefer traveling for trade and making a name and fame for themselves. However, two cards Ravana held at that time carried superior value compared to us. One of that was their advanced weapons. Apparently, they had a division of horse-drawn chariots. We in Aryavarta use horses for ceremonies and chariots for transporting people. Lankans likely imported the know-how from the land of Kemet where their Pharaohs rode atop chariots. Ravana's second card was his seasoned commanders. Word was that he had ten commanders, counting himself, that could be deployed to suit a particular type of battle. They were all very experienced, skilled, and all of them command the loyalty of their army and the trust of Ravana himself. Above all, most were his look-alikes, who could disguise themselves as Ravana and confuse the enemy. It was rumored that perhaps one of his look-alikes was in fact the person that kidnapped bhabhi. We may never know. Be that as it may, we needed to kill all ten of them. While this was going to be difficult for us to counter, it was probably also their weakness that we need to exploit. Such vital intelligence could be turned against them, as it made them very predictable. Ironically, our father was also called Dasa-ratha – the one who rode a chariot pulled by ten horses. A rarity back in Aryavarta. But among the Lanka commanders, the foremost of those was Ravana himself, followed by his brother – the giant brute Kumbakarna, and his son Meghananda – the mentalist and illusionist. Rumor had it that Ravana's other brother Vibheeshana is more of a pacifist and has been vocal about condemning the whole kidnapping episode.

Rama thought it was key for us to win him over to our side, and then extract finer intelligence details if we are to stand a chance.

The route we took was to first march down South to the plains in the old Tamil country, then sail down the coast and onwards further South before reaching a place called Dhanushkodi, near the Pamban coast. That place is so named as the strip of land resembles the middle-pointed portion of a bow. It was Jambavan who had figured out that the closest point to Lanka lay in Dhanushkodi. Apparently, there are natural land bridge formations that we can seek to fill, and then it is only two yojanas from there to a place called Talaimannar in Lanka. "Only" is a misplaced word. Neither do I know how we will buff up the land bridge to hold the weight of an entire marching army. The sea there is known to be unpredictable. We are just coming off the monsoons, so the waves may be less rough. Nevertheless, this is fraught with immense danger. Jambavan and Nala have worked out a way with their engineers. Rama was discussing with them the other day. Nala started talking about our ancient method of measurements and distances. I overheard him alluding to using some 4:2:1 golden ratio of geometry. And then I must have dozed off. This topic is always a cure for insomnia.

For that moment, I concerned myself with admiring the beauty of the river Kaveri in full flow and the lush green paddy fields lining either side of the blue river. After the rains, this was a sight to behold. Three weeks into the journey, we reached the ancient holy land near Pamban. Legend has it that Lord Rudra himself had stayed for a few years here. And we set up camp somewhere between Pamban and Dhanushkodi.

Map not drawn to scale

Over the next few days, Rama and Sugreeva spent most of their time with Nala and Nila up at the coast discussing the bridge. Jambavan had dispatched Hanuman to head to some place to fetch medicinal herbs for treating wounded soldiers. This was a mountain West of here in the Cheralam country. Apparently, Lord Rudra also spent some time there with Sage Agastya. This mountain has since been called Mahendragiri.

Angada and I were at the army camp overseeing the soldiers' equipment, conducting drills, and running mock battle formations.

If I didn't talk about Angada before, now is never too late. Angada was Vali's son, as I mentioned earlier. Sugreeva did the honorable thing after Vali's death and adopted Angada as his own son. He even arranged a quick ceremony to coronate him as the crown prince. Despite his objection, Angada insisted on joining us. This strapping young lad was full of vitality. He was also very skilled, and like all young boys, he liked to show off his talents by challenging some soldier or other to a duel. I suppose his father's fetish for duels rubbed off on Angada as well.

On that particular day, I went with Rama. He wanted me to help with material selection. This too was my twin brother Shatrugna's forte. I didn't consider myself as being good at constructing anything. Let alone some contraption of a bridge. But I wanted a break from the drills, so I gladly joined Rama. Nala had studied the tidal patterns and worked out the best time to lay the stones. But he felt that the sand couldn't be used and instead we needed different soil to be laid on the top of the rocks to level the path.

Did I ever mention the ingenuity of the Vanars and specifically their ability to adapt to their environment?

They could make use of locally available flora and fauna to suit their needs. That's right. Animals. They have trained animals of all kinds that they utilize to serve some specific purpose. If it's not birds to carry messages, then it is monkeys harassing the enemy. Today I am witnessing the most audacious of trained animals. Squirrels that could roll on soil and carry it to unreachable crevices and simply shake it off loose! And there were tens of thousands of these little ones scurrying about doing their business. I learned that you only have to train the leader squirrel. The rest take their cue from the leader and simply follow the action.

But the next few days were an amazing display of coordination, camaraderie, and cooperation between man, birds, animals, and, I daresay, the weather. Using an existing natural formation of limestone rocks that lined up on the shoal, Nala combined his amazing engineering knowledge with the coordinated effort of man and animals to build the most magnificent land bridge on the ocean. One of the soldiers called it Ram Setu, and the moniker stuck. The entire army was charged up and praised the name of Rama while vilifying Ravana in equal measure. If the almighty Lord Muruga is with us, Rama would vanquish the enemy that has ten commanders, just as our great ancestor Sudas defeated the dasa-rajnas. With the marching army and an unpredictable ocean, we didn't know how long this makeshift bridge would last, but I just hoped it stayed until we returned from Lanka. Assuming we would return victorious.

Ketu and I eventually set out from Kashi and proceeded to Malwa. Over the next several months, we had drawn up a plan for the short term and long term. In terms of our base, we set up a camp near some of the richest mining areas. We wanted to first establish the technological capability before turning to building cities and residences. With great support from Scholar Dumma, who was one of Guru Vashista's senior disciples, Ketu was progressing well in overseeing various activities.

Meanwhile, I had been communicating with Bharata and Hanuman on information regarding the Chyavanas. Bharata's men have not been able to dig up any new information. However, Hanuman communicated that he was expanding his watch to cover festivals and other community gatherings. He felt that social events were always the best breeding grounds for recruiting new members and propagating one's ideology. That was a smart move. For now, I continue to focus on my task, and that is, to assist Ketu in establishing Chandrakanti as a center of manufacturing.

Part 5 – Legacy of a
True Leader

|| Chintis Tu Unnade Yamudu ||

Chapter 15

Jambavan Sends an Urgent Message

Nearly a year has passed since we left Ayodhya. I was still in Chandrakanti, guiding Ketu. This past year has been hectic for us. Based on Hanuman's scouting reports, we landed at Chandrakanti in the Malwa region, which itself was an interesting choice. The majority of Malwa is on a plateau-like highland and is flanked on its West by the almost-dying Saraswati riverbeds, beyond which lies the ancient Aravalli range. To the South lies the Vindhya range, beyond which flows the great Narmada River. To the North of the Malwa plateau is the fertile Vidisha province, which hosts the great Yamuna River. The present-day Malwa region is sparsely inhabited barring a few scatterings of hamlets. But in the ancient past, when River Saraswati was in her majestic flow, this was a thriving place. Legend has it that in a place called Bimbetka, our ancients from over ten thousand years ago had lived in caves and left behind paintings and tools that added to the complex tapestry of the origin of life. Despite being a semi-arid region, this place has three great practical advantages. First, of course, there are rich deposits of non-stratified iron ore that enable relatively easier production of śyāma-ayas metal alloys. Secondly, there are several rivers that originate from this region. Because of the topography being a plateau, the soil is not fertile for agriculture, but the abundance of river streams allows for mining and transportation. Third, this place was close to the ancient Ahar-Banas region. That was regarded as the first place where iron was mined. The quality of iron was not great, but we are talking about a metal that was extracted almost a thousand years before. The Banas canal and the proximity to Saraswati River allowed those people to trade their finished tools. Most of the tools were used for minor agricultural and household purposes. But the trade route the Ahar-Banas people had established is still somewhat active, if not thriving. It was all these factors that made us target this specific place to establish as the city of *Chandrakanti*.

Within the first few months after we moved here, we built ramparts around the town settlement to allow for people to migrate and establish their residence. We cleared some of the forest lands to make way for roads. Tunnels were built by traditional rat miners to begin mining operations. We started making significant progress. Ketu was involved in all aspects of establishing the town and preparing the groundwork for mining production and transportation. Slowly but surely, Rama's vision of establishing a center of manufacturing was taking shape. Success begets success. Word had started spreading about our plans and we were starting to get trade inquiries from other kingdoms, and experts in metallurgy started knocking on our doors to ply their craft. While the whole scheme might take another two years to be fully operational, the next few months are crucial to establishing a strong foundation and announcing to the world that Kosala's reach, resources, and responsibilities were here to stay for several generations.

In parallel, I kept getting word from my brothers and from my other son, Angada, where similar plans were afoot to tap the resource-rich Kalinga forests. What the Malwa region was to the West, Kalinga was to the East. Both my sons have had a good start to their assignments. Likewise, Shatrugna and Bharata kept sending updates on progress by their sons. Apparently, Shatrugna's son Suvahu met some resistance from a local warlord called Lavanasura. So, that took a precious few months to overcome. Their goal of establishing Mathura as a key river port faced some delays, but my brother was confident that they would overcome that soon. Thus far, all our plans are mostly going okay.

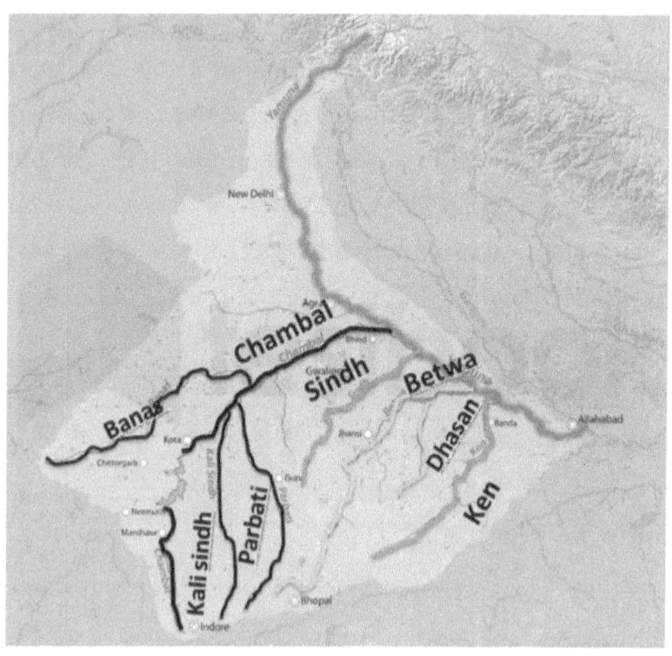

Perhaps I spoke too soon! A messenger came and handed me a sealed roll. It bore Jambavan's seal insignia of the boar. Jambavan stayed back in Ayodhya, assisting my brother Rama. So, if any communication had to reach me, it should have come from the official messenger, bearing our royal sun insignia. Instead, Jambavan chose to send a private message. Strange. I was in my tent, getting ready to go to a place to inspect the progress of a mine. That's right, I lived in a tent house. To avoid wasting precious resources and manpower to build palaces or houses for us, we first wanted to scout for the proper area to establish a township for the administrative and court staff before building housing for royals. But these tent houses were quite comfortable and spacious. Besides, should there be a need to move, it is much easier to dismantle tents and set them up where necessary. At the same time, these tents provided sufficient relief from the heat and dust that Malwa was known for.

I dismissed the messenger and opened the sealed roll. There was a short, small scroll with Jambavan's message that read: "Lord Lakshman, I am worried about Lord Rama. Something is not right. Come forthwith. Godspeed."

That was enough for me to drop all further plans for me in Chandrakanti. I quickly summoned Ketu and his senior adviser – Sage Dumma – and showed them the scroll and told them that I needed to get back to Ayodhya urgently. Sage Dumma was a senior disciple of Guru Vasishta and has been proving almost as brilliant as Guruji. Just before exiting, I turned back and looked at them in their eyes. Both just nodded and gave a signal for me to proceed without further thought. I knew they each understood that they had to keep this a secret – at least until I found out more details. After all, a king's health is not something you discuss freely.

I rode as fast as I could to reach Ayodhya to meet Rama. But before I could enter Ayodhya, a messenger intercepted and handed me a note. Again, a scroll bearing Jambavan's Boar insignia. It read: "Come to Rama's private place. Have informed others." I knew that the 'others' mentioned in that note refers to the members of the war Council. Outside of that, hardly anyone knows of this place's existence and even if they did, there wasn't much for anyone to connect the place with Rama. Since it is now mid-summer, it was not unusual for Rama to go there. However, the past year or so has been very busy for all of us, including him. So, I did not think he would have had the time to travel anywhere outside Ayodhya. Anyway, without further delays, I continued the road I was taking, bypassing the one that entered the city, and crossed Sarayu to reach the summer place, which is another half-day ride to the East of this road junction.

Even as I neared the vast sprawling grove surrounding this summer place, Jambavan was waiting for me, alone. I got down, hugged him briefly, and immediately enquired about Rama. He just slowly shook his head and said: "First, come inside the guest house, Lord Lakshman. Most others are here. Hanuman should reach here any minute now."

Even though I really wanted to meet Rama first, I dragged myself to follow Jambavan. He was right. If there are grave matters that concern the King and perhaps the kingdom, then it is best that we discuss them first. A collective action, rather than any impulsive move, seemed wise. I entered the guest house, which was definitely bigger and better furnished than Rama's own private house. I saw that Guru Vasishta and Sage Rishyasringa were already seated. Bharata was pacing the room impatiently. Shatrugna was standing by the window overlooking a stream. Due to this being summer, the water levels were low. But this was the same place we all last met over a year ago. As they say, 'much water has flowed…' Indeed, Shatrugna must be thinking about various events that have happened since that meeting. None of us would have imagined that we would assemble at the same place within a year or so. At one end of the room, Guruji and the Sage were calmly seated and were in meditation. Their long years of training and experience had given them the power and technique to focus on breathing to control thoughts and thereby control the mind which ultimately guides their action. My entrance hardly mattered to anyone there. The air was heavy with anticipation and anxiety. I too was not in a mood to engage in any light conversation. I touched the elders' feet to seek their blessings. Just in time too, as Hanuman walked in. The normally unflappable Hanuman looked worried. With his hirsute face, he looked like an aging lion that was relegated to loneliness. Jambavan gave a sound as if adjusting his voice. Everyone in the room looked up at me and Hanuman, but no one spoke.

I could not take this silence anymore. So, I spoke first: "Jambavan, it looks like we all received a similar message from you asking us to come here quickly. Surely, you would not have done that had something serious not happened. Pray tell us why we are here and how is brother Ram?"

Jambavan replied: "Lord Lakshman, the past few months have been very painful for me, and I am sorry for not requesting you all to come earlier. Had not my hands and tongue been tied by King Rama, I would have done so sooner."

Guruji intervened and said, "Dear Jambavan. Don't think back about what could have and should have happened. And don't blame yourself. Let's think about what we need to do now. Although I have some idea of what might be bothering you, even I have been away for the past several months. Why don't you fill us all in about your concerns first, and then we'll discuss the next steps?"

Jambavan replied: "Thank you, Guruji. Dear Council members, as you all know, last year, we embarked on realizing King Rama's vision of expanding this kingdom's reach to the four corners of Aryavarta and the young princes were assigned the primary responsibility to lead that effort. Those activities are also proceeding satisfactorily. The first few months, King Rama was very busy in planning as well as monitoring the progress. Hanuman and I have been mostly by his side, coordinating those efforts. However, something happened about six months back. He had a strange visitor, who asked to meet the King in private. This was not uncommon, as there is usually someone or other who wished to speak with the King in private. The first meeting was very short, and the visitor left immediately. The only strange thing was that the King accompanied him up to the gate to see him off. But then there was no word from this person for several days. So, I almost forgot about this incident. About a month later, he returned. Again, he requested a private audience with King Rama. The King seemed to have been expecting him, so this person was given a special pass to meet with him. This time, the meeting lasted a bit longer. Again, the King went with him up to the palace gates to see him off. This time, I sent one of my security guards to follow this person discreetly and report back. The guard came back later that day and said that the person went straight to the goddess Bhadra Kali temple on the north just outside the city and just rested there the whole night.

"As you know, there are some new sects that worship this goddess and their rituals are, so to speak, crude. They sacrifice animals, have body paint, and drink blood. Anyway, after three days, he returned and then kept coming every three days."

Bharata intervened and asked: "Jambavan, what was King Rama doing with this sect? Do you think this was his way of reaching out to tribals and being inclusive?"

"That's what I initially thought. But what bothered me is that King Rama's behavior gradually started changing," said Jambavan, and then he stayed quiet.

"Jambavan, don't hesitate. Speak freely. What behavioral change did you observe?" asked Sage Rishyasringa.

"Guruji, pardon me if I misspeak. But, in the past four or five months, the King's attention to our mission has been reducing. He started frequenting this Bhadra Kali temple alone. Also, he has started to speak to himself!" said Jambavan, hesitantly.

"What do you mean, 'speaking to himself?' Are you accusing my brother? Maybe he is indeed talking to someone. And, Hanuman, where have you been? Why haven't you arrested this person? You have all let down bhayya," roared Bharata.

"Bharata, my child, please calm down. Allow Jambavan to speak," Guruji counseled.

"Lord Bharata, please forgive me if I offended your sentiments. Who am I to say anything about our great King Rama? I am merely talking about the changes I've noted. He has started spending a lot of time alone, and periodically many of us have heard him speaking to himself, in his chamber. As for Hanuman, well, that is another strange thing. After the first visit, King Rama sent Hanuman to meet with Nagvanshis on the pretext of negotiating with them to part with their śyāma-ayas extraction technology. I say 'pretext' because it was after Hanuman left that the frequency of this person's visits started increasing. This cannot be a coincidence," replied Jambavan.

"Lord Bharata, indeed, I let Lord Rama down. If I had been around, I would not have allowed this mystic sorcerer anywhere near the King," lamented Hanuman.

I was now worried. First, we have Rama meeting some sorcerer. Then Rama sends Hanuman away, perhaps knowing that Hanuman would not allow such meetings. Then, the meeting frequencies increase. And then we have Rama's behavior and possibly state of mind in question. Jambavan did the right thing by calling us, but perhaps he could've done so much earlier. God, save my brother!

"Jambavan, are you sure Ram bhayya was not really talking to someone, who may have joined him without your knowledge? If not, why has the royal physician not been asked to diagnose him?" questions poured from Shatrugna.

After some hesitation, Jambavan replied: "Lord Shatrugna, the King spends a lot of time closeted in his chambers. But in many instances, his voice could be heard. And mostly he was talking to…," trailed off Jambavan.

I impatiently interrupted him and said: "Jambavan, we are like brothers. You know you can speak freely here. Who was he talking to?"

Jambavan looked at me at length, and without blinking he said in his hoarse voice: "He has been talking to you or our late Queen Sita devi."

I nearly lost my balance and had to hold on to a nearby pillar. I had tears in my eyes hearing this, as did my brothers. The calmest, most equanimous, speaker of truth, strict follower of Dharma and a man of one word, i.e., Rama, being delirious and losing his mind? Unbelievable.

After composing ourselves, Bharata said: "Okay, I'm done talking. Let us all go and speak with Rama, without any delay. What if he requires some medical assistance?" I too almost started to walk away from that room to meet Rama.

Jambavan held up his hands as if to stop him and said: "Lord Bharata, the King has given very strict orders to me to guard this place and not allow anyone to enter his private residence. And if someone were to do so, they would be banished forever from this kingdom. He was very particular on this point!"

I was exasperated and wondered aloud: "Banished? Who is this sorcerer that has been corrupting Rama's pure mind?"

Jambavan said: "I sent a few experienced spies to follow this person and uncover his background. He goes by the name Yama."

Even the normally unflappable Guruji was taken aback at the identity of this secret sorcerer and dreaded visitor, Yama. He had a reputation for heading a secret cult that allegedly worships Lord Rudra. But there have been stray incidents of unsuspecting youth, lonely men or women that have been hypnotized to join his cult. And no one has seen or heard from these individuals. But what was Rama doing with him? If somehow this Yama character had trapped Rama in his web, that would be a great win for his cult but a disaster for the Kosala Kingdom. We must put a stop to this.

Hanuman finally got the answer that he was looking for over a year. The leader of the Nagvanshis, who was instigating the Chyavanas to trade their metal craft with people outside of Kosala, was none other than Yama. The audacity, surreptitiousness, and boldness with which he has been meticulously operating right under our nose is just mind boggling. A part of me felt it was not too late. We might not have caught Yama, but for over a year, we too have been preparing to meet any challenge. Even as we were deciding our next course of action, a soldier rushed in with an urgent message to Jambavan. Apparently, the famous scholar Durvasa was arriving in Ayodhya later today and had sent word that upon his arrival, he wished to get an audience with King Rama immediately!

Chapter 16

Rama's Encounter with Yama

This was most unexpected. We did not have the time nor energy to welcome any dignitaries. That too, at a time when we were ourselves wondering how to extricate ourselves and specifically Rama out of Yama's net. That said, Durvasa Atriputra is not just any visitor. He is a scholar par excellence. He is the present leader of the ancient clan of Turvasus, who have fought against the Nagvanshis in the past. The Turvasus have been our allies and there have been several marriages between our people over time. Durvasaji himself was a very learned and respected scholar and over the past few years devoted his energy to teaching, traveling and advising anyone that sought him. However, the tempestuous nature of his clan makes you want to keep them at a distance. They can be whimsical and quirky. One day they are your best friends. The same day they can be your sworn enemies. This clan has also produced fierce warriors. Durvasaji is notorious for his temper. In short, it is easier and best to keep him in good humor. Imagine my astonishment when I learned that this very same man wanted to meet Rama. Of all days, Durvasaji chose this day to visit us? On the one hand, if we delay in getting Rama to meet with him, he is likely to curse us with all his might, causing a public display of his emotions. He can embarrass anyone without remorse. On the other hand, we cannot simply send any messenger inside the private chamber lest the poor chap incurs Rama's wrath.

It is this dilemma that confronted us. I raised my hands and declared to everyone in that room that I would go and speak to Rama myself. I argued that if Rama was referring to me and Sita bhabhi in his monologue, there is a chance that he may listen to me. The other thing is, I've had enough of this situation that I find myself in. I am too old for that now. I decided that even a severe punishment such as banishment is not going to bother me. Rama's health and wellbeing and the kingdom's future are more important than mine. Who knows? Maybe this is a good retirement package! I shall go West to the land of our ancestors, walk along the dry beds of the erstwhile great River Saraswati, and visit some pilgrim spots. It took a little bit more convincing on my part, but eventually everyone agreed with my decision, albeit reluctantly. With strength in my mind, and hope of getting the old Rama back, in my heart, I went to Rama's residence, alone.

I went to the side window of Rama's residence, from where I could not see him clearly but could hear him talking to himself: "Sita, this is not the time to play sister-in-law. Besides, I already spoke to them, and they are showing no interest in ruling. They refused on the grounds that they are also getting old. I agree. We need to think of the future. Our allies are also asking me the same."

I sensed that Rama was talking to bhabhi's golden statue. As I quietly peeked inside through the window, I could see that bhabhi's contented all-knowing smile gave comfort to Ram and made him pause.

He continued talking: "But, but..." Rama countered with a clenched fist. It looked like he was frustrated just referring to the word 'allies,' perhaps. Powerful clans they may be, but weak they are in courage. "There are murmurs, Sita! All that our allies want is to secure their positions within the *Janapada* hierarchy." *Ahgh*! Rama immediately bit his tongue.

Ram glanced at her statue and met Sita's eyes, which had the familiar I-told-you-so look. "Yes, yes, you had warned me and your father about the inherent difficulties of the Janapada system. But you know I had no other choice," said Rama with a shrug.

When Rama was crowned as king of Ayodhya two decades ago, he inherited a kingdom that had a leadership vacuum. Prior to that, during our fourteen years in the forest, Bharata was the acting ruler, but he decided to place Rama's slippers on the throne of Ayodhya and instead he himself ruled as a regent from a nearby town called Nandigrama. While he did an admirable job, the lack of leadership in the capital city made several people leave Ayodhya. Not only that, but our society was also already weakened, primarily due to the decade-long proxy war against the forces of Lanka. During our youth, Lanka was ruled by Ravana, but he had his proxy agents, his half-brother Visravana, and various other Lanka warlords operating out of a hideout that belonged to Ravana's uncle. A few years later, we found out that this hideout was in the forests, South of Ayodhya. Fighting these people constantly depleted our resources. Ultimately, when our father and Emperor Dasharatha passed away, the army Rama inherited was much weakened, the treasury nearly drained, and Ayodhya had also lost much of its intellectual capital.

Subsequently, when Rama took the kingship, he had turned to King Janaka's counsel on various aspects of administration. King Janaka, Sita bhabhi's father, had come up with a brilliant suggestion to formally establish a republic of kingdoms, with Ayodhya as the natural lead kingdom. The beauty of this system was to bring various kingdoms from descendants of the legendary King Bharata under one umbrella, yet allowing each to rule their territory with near autonomy. They would come together if there was any threat from an external foe, and they were free to govern and expand their territories as long as they didn't fight with each other.

While this was not a new concept, for there had been such republics in a much smaller capacity but less well defined. They were called 'gana-padas.' But when King Janaka redefined this, Guru Vasishta gave the name 'jana-padas.' This was partially in honor of King Janaka, and partially to mean that real power was placed at the foot of the people and not the ruling class.

Sita bhabhi, however, sounded caution to this system. She felt her father's republican-style governance would expose the fault lines within the various kingdoms. After all, she knows the male ego all too well. She reasoned that there might be a time in future when some king could use whatever reason to pick a quarrel with another king. This would blow up into a war. Or, she felt, we could experience a situation where a kingdom with no male heir would become subservient to another kingdom if there was a marriage alliance between them. Or worse, even a scenario where some subset of these kingdoms formed a confederacy among themselves and challenged

Ayodhya. Everyone knew all too well the epic war of the Dasa-rajnas – where our ancestor King Sudas Paijavana fought against a combined army of ten kings led by the Puru clan. And no one wanted a repeat of that. Territorial claims, competition for scant resources, and simply one-upmanship were invariably the reasons for war. This land, or Bharata Desa, was too diverse and fragile for this. After several rounds of discussion and fine-tuning, Rama went with a system that worked and it has been functioning well for several decades. Or was it that the system worked because of Rama? He was after all universally loved and respected, and no king dared challenge him.

I digress. I am getting old; my mind is wandering off with too many thoughts and I must somehow convey this urgent news of Durvasaji's arrival to Rama. I sensed a break in this monologue, so I quickly went to the main door, then knocked on it and tried opening it noisily. Rama hurried back to the main hall, saw me, stopped, and simply glared at me.

"Have you forgotten my explicit orders, Lakshmana?" Rama thundered in a cold voice.

I simply froze. I have never seen him this angry, certainly not with me. He was also pale, his long hair let loose, and he looked terrifying. I looked down at the floor and responded: "Brother, Scholar Durvasa is arriving in Ayodhya and has demanded to see you as soon as possible. Disrespecting him would affect our city. I decided that the alternative of facing your punishment was better."

Rama was thoughtful for a while. He just stared at me, breathing steadily. I stayed quiet till his tone relaxed. His eyes turned moist and red. It looked like he came back to reality. He said, in his normal voice: "Decided, eh? You know what this means to you, don't you, brother?"

He calls me 'brother' only when…. wait, he hasn't called me that since the war in Lanka when I was nearly fatally injured by Ravana's son Meghananda. At that time, well, I was unconscious, yes. But later I learned that Rama had wept uncontrollably and was awake nursing me till I regained consciousness. And right now, I am not dying. Ah, right! My banishment would cause him a big embarrassment, a blot to our family name and in all a moral dilemma for him to face. Worse than death, I think. But then, I would not allow him to treat me any more differently than he would any ordinary citizen of our kingdom Kosala. Rules are rules.

I wiped a bit of tears that had swelled in my eyes, took off my royal headdress and replied in a formal tone: "My Lord Rama. I am fully aware that I will be banished from Ayodhya. I would want nothing less. I shall comply with the order immediately. Please grant me leave." Surprisingly, I felt light after saying that. It was as if a huge burden was off my mind. By placing my headdress in his hands, I felt as if I was transferring the burden of carrying the administration of this kingdom, the burden of protecting the name of Rama, the lifetime burden of upholding Dharma. In a flash, I felt like my life's purpose on Earth was fulfilled.

Rama leaned over, hugged me, and held me tight for several moments and sobbed. I placed my head on his chest and felt the immense tension in my shoulders vanish. Urmila had left this world a few years back, just a couple of years after Sita bhabhi's demise. My sons, along with my nephews, are each leading their own territories. To fill the void ever since Urmila's demise, I had immersed myself in administering various projects on behalf of Ayodhya. Now, I don't need to do that anymore. But this moment was even more special. My mind started becoming clear. I knew what I wanted to do. I would go on a pilgrimage. I would then go up to the Himalayas, where I would spend the remainder of my days in meditation and frugal living. But before that, I need to make sure Rama is feeling normal and that he is free from any other dangerous elements. I need to carefully get him to fully trust us all and help him come out of Yama's trap. And with a little medical care and attention, we can get his old self back.

As all these emotions and thoughts were running through my mind, Rama released me from his embrace and spoke to me gently, "I am lucky to have you as my brother. I couldn't be prouder of your unwavering loyalty and commitment to upholding Dharma. In fact, even as I was not myself these past few months, I frequently got strange visions in my dreams. It was as if I already knew this was going to happen, very clearly. It was as if you and I were in a battle over evil. It was as if we had done this before, several times. And it felt like I was getting a message that our work is done and we have to leave. What can you make of it? When did we do all this before? Where do I leave from here? I am not able to explain. Initially, I myself dismissed these as just dreams. But they have been coming over and over.

However, leave all that aside. There is a lesson to be learned from your act, by our sons. The citizens of Saketa must hear about this. Our great republic of Aryavarta must hear about this. Let not the lineage of our ancestor Ikshvaku ever be denounced for ignoring Dharma. However, don't go. I forgive you, Lakshmana."

I looked him closely in his eyes, wiped tears from my own and said: "Brother, I do not know how to explain your dreams. Maybe it is some effect of Yama's sorcery. Maybe it is age. But on a much smaller scale, I too have been feeling a strange sense of accomplishment for some purpose. My only purpose that lived and believed has been that 'your word is my command.' Now, if everyone has to hear about my act, then they should also know that King Rama's one word is Dharma and that he does not change his word. If you forgive me now, this stain shall forever stay with our clan. Therefore, please allow me to leave the kingdom. But first please tell me what happened to you? Who is this Yama?"

Rama, almost back to his old self, spoke in his usual measured tone: "Yes, I am sorry. I owe you an explanation. A few months back this person, Yama, came to meet me. It was a brief meeting in which he lamented that he and his followers were being persecuted simply for practicing an ancient and rather mysterious worship of Shakti. He pleaded with me to support them in their cause, lest this come as a blot on an otherwise utopian kingdom of ours. I weighed his words and considered his petition. But there was something about him that drew me in, which I didn't realize then. Initially, I paid no more attention than a token support of granting them funds to refurbish their temple. He came back after a few weeks and this time he requested me to join in their consecration ceremony. He mentioned that despite my funds and support, our soldiers posted near that area were harassing them repeatedly. Thus, he felt my presence would send a message once and for all. Besides, by this time, I had assigned someone to validate this story, which checked out. So I reluctantly agreed to participate in their ceremony. But Yama visited me often on some pretext or other. Each time, however, I started realizing that I was drawn to their way of worship. I could sense passion, faith, absolute devotion, selfless sacrifice, utmost respect for nature, fewer rituals, and more self-discovery of oneself. Anyway, I went to their village, which was on the outskirts of Ayodhya, and not too far from this summer retreat. Somehow he had convinced me that I should go there once, before the actual consecration ceremony, not as a King but as an ordinary individual. He made me believe that this would allow me to see for myself their way of faith. And inexplicably I found myself agreeing with this. Their rituals were strange, at times bizarre. I won't say they were tribals, as there were people of all kinds. Some from around here, some from Dravida desa, and some from kingdoms much to the East of Aryavarta. But what seemed to unite all these people was their common belief and faith in a nature-based worship. They had a goddess-looking figurine, which they called Bhadra Kali. The idol was taller than us, placed on a pedestal, made of clay and painted in black. The decorations were simple. The bizarre part that shocked me was that the idol's garland was made of skulls. The tongue of the goddess was sticking out. Her eyes were painted in red and white with the eyeballs staring at you. This was very mesmerizing and powerful. Their temple was not a closed structure, rather a large open courtyard with no restrictions on who can go near the statue. While some people were making arrangements for the upcoming consecration ceremony, most followers seemed to be in a state of trance and simply singing and dancing. Yama was their chief and he seemed to have a large following. There were priests, of course, but they too were busy with preparations for the ceremony. There seemed to be no rules, no restrictions and no order. Yet, there was no chaos. I found this aspect, of having an open society with each allowed to do their own thing, appealing. The most shocking aspect that Yama told me was that on the day of the function, there would be people walking on fire or even those willing to sacrifice their lives. Their belief is in absolute surrender to their goddess Kali, which will take them to a state of nirvana, where their life becomes free from the encumbrance of suffering. So if they cannot achieve that in this life, they sacrifice their life. It was this that I found most disturbing. While I don't know what to make of all this, I think Yama had been systematically manipulating my mind. Now that I think about it, I suspect he may have had an ulterior motive. And he perhaps has been poisoning the minds of innocent people. Anyway, I came back that night very disturbed. I needed someone to talk to. I did not have you around either. So I came over to this summer place to talk to Sita."

Rama took a pause as he seemed to be pondering on something, so I did not interrupt him. He continued: "Let this be a forgotten chapter in my life, Lakshmana. For a few months now, I seemed to have lost myself. Perhaps being alone without you all, or perhaps the burden of the future of our Kosala Kingdom, or perhaps age has allowed characters like Yama to exploit my fragility and weakness."

I replied: "Rama, do not despair. The hallmark of your leadership has always been that you are fully conscious of your own vulnerabilities. But we can investigate further the true background of Yama and find his ulterior intentions. I shall inform Hanuman, who will ensure that Yama and his cult followers are arrested. Now, please get ready. The sun is already starting to go down. You need to head back to Ayodhya quickly and welcome Durvasaji. If you permit, I shall accompany you there and then I shall leave tomorrow."

Rama looked at me with brotherly love and a sense of relief and said: "Lakshmana, I know Hanuman. He would do whatever it takes to protect me. Let him investigate the background of Yama. I don't think Yama and his band of followers are powerful. If he wanted to kill me, there were so many opportunities to have done that. I think he merely wanted to recruit and convert me into following their way of life. Maybe he wanted us to grant them exclusive trading rights with which they can easily control the overland trade we have with Ch'in or our Far-Western Kingdoms. I do not want to carry the blemish of being prejudiced and intolerant of alternate views. Let our society be a multicultural, multi-faith society. Only then will we learn and grow from each other. However, everyone must adhere to our Dharma and the rule of law. Yama does not have the right to take another person's life. Therefore, I banish him and his cult followers from our kingdom. Leave the other innocent people out of this. Tell this to Hanuman."

At this point, I was so thankful to the almighty for granting my Rama back to us. Perhaps there was something I said or our embrace that released him from being in a state of trance. Whatever happens to me now pales in comparison. It was time to go back to Ayodhya, perhaps for the last time.

Chapter 17

Durvasa warns of a Threat from Abroad

Normally, when a scholarly person such as Durvasa comes, they are welcomed as per Ayodhya tradition whereby the entire family washes their feet as well as that of their disciples, places garlands on them, and performs a small ritual to ward off their travel tiredness. This time he came with just one attendant, and he seemed to be in a hurry. He waved off the aarti and welcoming party and merely asked to see Rama.

Bharata, Shatrugna and I, along with Hanuman and our Guru Vasishta, waited outside the royal gates to receive the sage. The only person he acknowledged was Hanuman, with a slight nod at Guruji. I exchanged a glance with my brothers at this unusual entry. On the other hand, Guruji seemed to have understood the situation and nodded to us to act as per Durvasa's wishes.

Anyway, we accompanied Durvasaji to meet with Rama, silently. We were mostly quiet as we knew better than to start any small talk as that would incur a wrath or worse, expletives and choice expletives. Rama came outside the hall and touched his feet in reverence. Together they both entered the chambers. Rama signaled us to stay outside. Guruji had stayed back at the palace. Rama was closeted with Durvasaji for a long time in the visitor's hall. Whatever he wanted to discuss must have been quite urgent and important. For as soon as they finished their discussions, both stepped out of the private visitor's and immediately called us to convene the Inner Council of ministers. Bharata had already planned for that, sensing an impending meeting of importance. It was agreed that we would not mention Yama or Rama's health and rather strictly restrict the agenda to discuss the news Durvasaji had brought with him. We did not know the details, other than the fact that Rama sent a quick word that there is a matter of security that needs discussion.

Accordingly, Rama had invited Durvasaji to join the assembly proceedings. This was not unusual, as occasionally, our Council meetings would have a special invitee. Guru Vishwamitra, Sage Agastya, the wandering oracle Narada, Lanka King Vibheeshana, Kishkinda King Sugreeva, and now his adopted son King Angada, et al., are some of the notable personalities that have graced us with their presence in the past. Although Durvasaji's arrival has caused my eventual banishment, I hold no ill-will toward him. Usually, he has the right intentions, and his actions eventually do more good than harm. So maybe there is some good from all this. In fact, all this while since my meeting with Rama, I haven't had any feeling of being at the receiving end. Rather, as I mentioned earlier, I was looking forward to retiring in peace. Just as I was having these thoughts, Bharata rose to speak:

"Ram bhayya. We have been successful in expanding Kosala's reach. However, as the head of security, I have failed in anticipating this new threat to our security that you alluded to in your note earlier today. To seek redemption, I would like to put a final stop to that. Who is this enemy? Where do they originate from?" Such questions poured from the irrepressible Bharata.

Rama offered a faint smile at this outburst, to an otherwise somber atmosphere, and replied: "Bharata. Let no one ever tell you that you have failed in your duty. Ever since our vanavasa – exile in the forest – you have protected this throne, our people, and our borders admirably. If this important piece of intelligence has evaded you, it is because it is a new emerging risk. One that, if left uncontrolled, can come to damage us. I too was made aware of this only today. And the bearer of such important information is none other than the great scholar Durvasa. And the main reason why he is our honored guest today is so that we could all hear from his own words. I now request Durvasaji to share what he knows. Hear him out first. We shall discuss the next steps later."

Aha! Now this sudden visit and a sense of urgency makes sense. Durvasaji is a much sought-after individual. He knows the land near and afar, he knows people of all kinds, he can speak well over a dozen languages. To me, he is someone who just knows everything there is to know. Many merchants take him with them on their voyages and trade missions. Not just as a translator, but the man has a glib tongue that has a knife on one edge and ice on the other. He can negotiate your own self to you for a price, just as easily as he can make you hate yourself! Frequently kings from other parts of the world invite him for advice and consultation. And this unfettered access gives him vital information. While he plays his cards close to his chest, he does share with us a hatred for the ilk of Ravana. His own Turvasu clan has been a victim of the machinations of Ravana and Nagvanshis. But that was all in the past. Or so I thought. What is he worried about now? Hmm, more questions than I could fathom answers to.

Durvasa rose and, after the usual salutations to everyone, turned toward Guru Vasishta and spoke:

"I am just coming from the distant land of Mittani, where I have presided over a peace treaty between them and their neighbors, the Hittites. They have both taken a solemn pledge to cease all hostilities and have taken an oath in the name of our deities Indra, Mitra and Varuna. Subsequently, I have also been called by the King of the land of Kemet to advise on some matter of importance that concerns their state. Their kings are addressed as the Pharaohs. Their land, as you might have heard, is famous for giant stone buildings which they call the Pyramids. My ship sails in a few days. I don't have a whole lot of time for bureaucratic debates and public opinion seeking. The information I have has the power to make or break the future of Ayodhya."

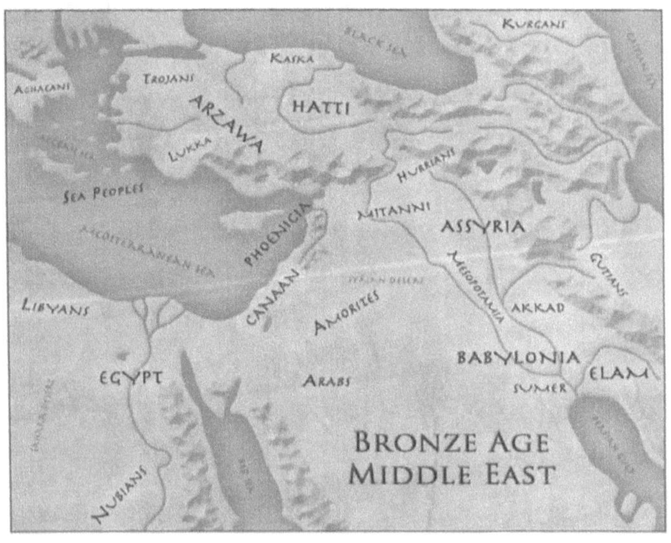

Whew! A greater dramatis personae you can't find elsewhere. On a different day, at a different time, I might have had the sense of humor to respond. Today was not the day for him to show off how important and valuable his time is.

Mercifully, Guru Vasishta replied: "My friend Durvasa, none of us have any doubt that you are foremost among all the learned scholars. Stories of your travel adventures and successes do reach us from time to time. However, clearly you have something that concerns Ayodhya which you wish to share. We are eager to hear you and act as per your counsel." Any amount of butter would melt in Guruji's gift of the gab.

Durvasaji continued, after mellowing down considerably: "You are right, my friend Vasishta. What I have learned recently has agitated me so much. I realize you may not be privy to that information, so let me give you the details. The land of Kemet is ruled by a young valiant king whom they call the Pharaoh. He has recently successfully completed wars, signed peace treaties, and consolidated political power in a few short years. However, he is facing an enemy from the sea for the first time. I too have encountered this earlier in our trade mission to the island of Knossos, a year back. They are ruthless people and are very skilled in sea-based battles. They do not seem to be interested in capturing any land. Rather, they come, destroy you, plunder you and then, just as noisily, leave you to lick your own wounds. Their attacks are vicious, sudden, yet efficient. Not too different from that of our Northern land-based barbaric Mleccha tribes. The Pharaoh has an excellent, battle-ready army. But he feels that it is no good to meet this danger from the sea. I am one of the few that have encountered these people and lived to talk about it. Hence the call from the Pharaoh."

Jambavan intervened at this stage and thundered: "Ha! I have faced these pirate types in Lanka and have thrashed them. What is unique about these Sea Savages? And pray, wise Durvasa, what has that got to do with us here, a thousand yojanas from Kemet? Do they want our assistance?"

The Sage looked at him with some pity and responded: "Tch, tch, tch… my dear Jambavan. Experienced as you may be, battle-scarred as you may be, you haven't faced an enemy that has boats that can travel underwater in stealth. You haven't seen these people that don't have any loyalty to anyone or anything other than gold. No. The most interesting part is this mercenary group are from no place in particular and are not all the same race nor do they speak the same language even. It is as if they are a group of mercenaries from various parts of the world that have assembled just to gain wealth by plundering. What more, I have information from a reliable source that a sizable section of these people speak Dravida bhasha!"

Now that is some news! Our brethren from the South as mercenaries operating that far away? And fighting Kemet by drawing them out to sea? I am sure none of us in the hall could fathom such a thing. A naval battle? By our people? If word of this spreads out, it could cause damage to the ties we have with all the major powers in that part of the world. The Kemet, Hittites, Mittanis, Elamites and Minoans are all our trade partners. They have been for several centuries. If they think that we are somehow involved in their internal politics, that could cause our trade relations to collapse. Worse, they could retaliate somehow. Equally grave is the fact that our army and resources are already stretched thin with us expanding our frontiers. I am sure Rama thought through all this as Durvasaji shared this information earlier today.

Bharata spoke: "Respected Durvasaji. What you have just shared is a matter of grave concern indeed. I can see why, with your knowledge of Dravida bhasha and their local language, plus your firsthand experience of encountering these sea peoples – as you call them – the Pharaoh of Kemet would have requested your counsel. But what I don't understand is, why did you mention an old enemy resurfacing? As far as I know, ever since the Lanka war, we have been having an excellent relationship with Dravida Kingdoms. Do you suspect one of them to have gone renegade?"

The Sage replied: "My boy. No offense, but our Dravida Kingdoms are too small for such an act, even though they all are adept at sea trade. Besides, they don't gain anything this way. They already have excellent trade relationships with Kemet. Anything against that would be like killing the proverbial golden goose."

Bharata asked: "Exactly. So, who then is this enemy from our own Southern kingdoms?"

"Ah, and yes, you mention the Lanka war. Let me ask you, who do you think was defeated in that battle?"

Bharata replied: "As any child in Ayodhya knows, it was Ravana and his entire family and army."

A sort of cross-examination was being conducted next between them both.

"Did no one survive?"

"Other than our trusted ally the wise King Vibheeshana, I can't think of anyone."

"What about Ravana's sister?"

"Surpanaka? Didn't she get humiliated by my brother Lakshmana and run away? I assume she must've gone mad and died by now."

"Do you manage security details for Ayodhya by 'assuming' things, my boy?"

This ticked Bharata off and he retorted: "Our forces are some of the best trained, and I am confident we can face any enemy from sea, land, or air!"

Rama intervened right then and said: "Stop this, both of you! I shall not have dissent among us. Durvasaji, kindly do not pay attention to the last comment from my brother. I know you mean well, but please get on with who you think is the enemy and how we can prepare ourselves."

Clearly, Rama was reminded of the past from the last comment about an attack from the 'air.' Several years back, Ravana had glided his way into our ashram in the forest and then tied up Sita bhabhi to get quickly to his ship that was anchored on the banks of the River Pampa. He used a contraption – which we later found out in Lanka – that was called a glider. This was essentially a wooden triangular three-dimensional frame with two wing-like sub-frames attached, making it look like a giant bird. The bottom of this frame allowed for up to two individuals to strap themselves in position. This frame was dismantlable, making it very easy to carry anywhere. The whole frame structure was wrapped with a fine thin cloth. This material was at that time unknown to us, but apparently, the Lankans obtained it through their trade with a far Eastern Kingdom of Shang. They called it silk. The way it worked was you would strap yourself to the frame, situate yourself atop a hill or mountain, and then just jump. Based on the wind direction, you could maneuver your landing spot. This offered a quick way to reach valleys and ravines, effectively allowing you to cover very long distances quickly. What could take several days could be reached in a couple of hours. It does come with disadvantages. One, this only works in mountainous regions. Also, it is best done in the dark. Otherwise, you are an easy prey to enemy arrows. Third, if the frame breaks, well, you're out of luck. All said, Ravana and some of his close aides were adept in using this. Our Sita bhabhi was a victim to this, unfortunately. Ravana also had the silk cloth painted in beautiful patterns and colors to make it look like either Garuda – the legendary bird, or a strange Ch'in beast that the Shang people called a 'dragon,' or like a fire-breathing snake. This also scared the enemy soldiers or people that they frequently harassed. Of course, when we won the Lanka war, King Vibheeshana renamed it as 'Pushpaka Vimana' and painted the fabric in flower patterns. He banned its use for military purposes. Instead, it was repurposed for providing medical assistance or disaster management to remote areas quickly. He also lent a few to us to quickly get back to Ayodhya after the war.

This saved a considerable amount of time on our way back. Now then, we never could replicate this aerial weapon nor really use it as there weren't too many hills around Ayodhya. Ironically, some child thought of taking a piece of this silk cloth, stuck it to a small frame of sticks, tied a rope at its end, and let it waft in the air. That little toy was called a 'kite' and became more popular than the original Pushpak! All in all, it was understandable that Rama became petulant when Bharata mentioned 'enemy attacking from air.'

After this, the Sage continued: "My apologies to Lord Rama. Anyway, continuing where I left, you all knew the myth surrounding Ravana was that he had ten heads and twenty arms. Subsequently, you realized that the myth came about because Ravana had ten, including him, that looked nearly exactly like him. He made it appear that he could appear in one place one day and appear in another far-off place the next day, building on this myth. And besides his brother Kumbakarna and son Meghananda, he had powerful and loyal followers. Most of them were killed in the Lanka battle at the hands of Lord Rama. However, not all of them died back then. Ravana's nephew from his elder sister is none other than Lavanasura – the same 'warlord' that Shatrugna, here, and his son defeated recently. Ravana's younger sister Surpanaka escaped from Lanka with a few trusted men, soon after

Ravana's defeat. And don't you think for one moment that Ravana's half-brother Visravana was banished by Ravana either, a few years prior to the war. They both patched up soon after Ravana took control of the Kingship of Lanka."

The deal was that Visravana would protect their merchant ships that were trading in far-off places from pirates. He commanded a dedicated large naval fleet. After the death of Ravana, all of these renegade forces united under the banner of the Nagvanshis. Their stated purpose was to wreak havoc in Aryavarta and defeat Kosala. They dispersed to various parts of the known world, often supporting each other. They were biding their time, partly because they were still weak, but partly also because Lord Rama has been providing strong leadership over the past two decades.

Anyway, over time several leaders died. Surpanaka too died somewhere alone, having gone mad with rage. That was the last straw for the old Lanka. Or so I thought. But a few years back they regrouped and amalgamated themselves as part of the sea peoples. Thus the Dravida language speaking section within those pirates whom I encountered. So, now, imagine a situation where they cause damage to Kemet, just as they did to Knossos and others. They get an easy route to Bharata Desa from our Western ocean. Not only that, but they also have the means to control the trade network, disrupting the flow of goods from Kemet to Lanka with Bharata Desa in between. With this, three things will happen:

First, they will destroy our economy, then capture political power and finally target our society itself. And all your plans for expanding into other frontiers will suffer.

Second, they will collude with, if not already done so, Yama using the old Nagvanshi connection.

Third, they will find a way to steal your weapons technology and know-how.

Don't look surprised, Bharata. I have my sources everywhere. So, I know that śyāma-ayas weapons are going to be the future. And if I know, rest assured, those pirates also know. In a way, this is from Ravana's old playbook – surround you from outside and spread from within!"

Chapter 18

Rama's Final Orders

There was absolute silence in the hall. Durvasaji went and sat back in his seat, combing his beard and smiling at his own brilliance. After a little while, the members started talking to someone next to them and trying to discuss the next steps. Rama was somber and thoughtful through all this, and finally stood up: "Thank you, wise Durvasaji. You have done us an enormous favor by bringing this timely information. Grave as it may be, but if we act now, we can be prepared. And this need not affect our plans for succession or expansion. Respected Durvasaji, I request you to let Hanuman accompany you to Kemet. His ability to penetrate any enemy territory and wreak havoc from within is unparalleled. Jambavan, I trust you with mustering a crack unit of naval soldiers and preparing them to infiltrate among the sea peoples. They need to gather intel and be able to assist the Pharaoh of Kemet. They will communicate only with Hanuman and no one else. Of course, they need to be able to know very basic words of the Kemet language. Bharata, I would need you now more than ever, to oversee the surveillance on Yama and prevent any groupings. Anyone disobeying should be thrown out of our kingdom. Meanwhile, Shatrugna, I need you to monitor all our sons' progress and assist them in every possible way." Rama was all business. Our problems were apparent. And our way ahead was now very clear. But the old Rama was back!

Each member in the Council had a specific objective but was bound by one objective: a pre-emptive strike on Ayodhya's enemies to ward off external threats and prepare the grounds for succession to secure our future. Although that was the end of the discussion, neither did Rama sit back on his throne nor were the members keen to disperse. Rather, most of them turned toward me, and then at Rama, and back at me. Naturally, they felt that it was odd that I didn't speak. Rama looked at me, pain written all over his eyes, but his stoic frame and eyes didn't give way to any emotions. With a resolute voice, he announced his decision to banish me from Kosala and explained very briefly the reason why he had put out an order like that. I know Rama. He goes by the book and the rules are clear. Durvasaji turned and looked at me, his eyes conveying a sense of apology. Bharata and Shatrugna appealed to Rama to reconsider. They argued that now was not the time to show our enemies that we are weakened.

Even as everyone was airing their views, Rama slowly turned towards me and spoke, as if addressing others: "All my life, Anuja here has been my dear brother and my right hand. Yet, we all know and understand why he must leave. He will not be missed because he is my heartbeat. I will not leave him alone for he is my soul, he is my shadow. He has to leave because none of us are bigger than our Dharma. But that Dharma allows me, the King, to grant anything he wishes to take."

I looked up at him and without batting my eyelid, I replied: "Grant me your slippers, oh King."

As I walked back to my room, I reflected on the last three days. Rama has gone through emotional tribulations throughout his life, yet he has never swerved from his duty to uphold the law of the land. I wished for his final few years to be peaceful, but in a way, I was responsible for bringing him more sorrow. In that sense, I am glad the whole incident came to a satisfactory closure. My only misgiving was that I couldn't assist in this shadow-war that we were undertaking. Rama continued to amaze me by having clarity of thought even in such trying times. How many kings are subjected to having to take simultaneous decisions – one affecting him personally, the other affecting his kingdom, and yet another impacting his future successors? Even at this advanced age, Rama continued to demonstrate the powers of compartmentalizing his thought process. Taking each decision on its own merit, delegating where necessary, and taking charge when required. Perhaps in a small way I can do some justice by teaching young children about leadership, values, and Dharma. Narrating incidents from Rama's life, just as I did with my sons and nephews, can be lessons in themselves for all generations to come. I know where I will go first. I will travel to the most ancient of our ancestors' places, by the dry wetlands of where the old River Saraswati flowed. This place is mostly in ruins, but there are legends abound about the greatness and vastness of the bygone era. The name of that place is *Hari-uppa*, or as they call it nowadays, **Harappa!**

Glossary

Term	Description
Names	
akka	sister
baba	Father
bhabhi	sister-in-law
bhayya	Brother
chacha	Uncle
chachi	Aunt
dada	Father
devarji	respected brother-in-law
didi	elder sister
Guruji	Respected Teacher

Term	Description
Pharaoh	The Egyptian rulers were addressed as Pharaohs, who were considered as above humans but below Gods
Raghu-vamsa	Dynasty of Ikshvakus, named after a subsequent King Raghu, who was an ancestor of Rama
Raj-Dharma	Kingly duties
Rajan and Praja	King and Subjects, respectively
spash	spies, in Sanskrit
Aadu-Puli-Attam	The Tamil/Telugu name for Goats (Aadu) and Tigers (Puli) Board Game (Aattam), considered by many to have originated in South India
anustubh metre and tristubh metre	Two of the most commonly used metres in the composition of Rig Veda, Valmiki Ramayan, Gayatri mantra and several shlokas
Ashram	Living quarters of Rishis

Term	Description
Ashvameda ritual	Ancient ritual involving the practice of letting loose a sacrificial horse. The regions it covers would be annexed by the King conducting this ritual. Any other king can challenge this in battle, by grabbing the horse
Bhasha	Language
Brahmastra	astra' means weapon. So, literally, weapon of Lord Brahma
Desa	Country
Dharma	No exact English equivalent for this word. But approximately signifies 'code of conduct'
dolmen	A stone structure that was very common from the Neolithic and Early Bronze age times which were used to bury or simply honor important dead persons
Gurukul	Ancient residential schooling system where students stayed with their teacher's household, for few years, till they completed their education

Term	Description
Janapada and Mahajanapada	Loosely translated as Republics. First finds mention in 6th BCE texts
Manusmiriti	literally, the code of Manu
paridesh, krosha, yojana, dhanush	Ancient Measurement of Units; 1 paridesh = 125 feet, approx 1 krosha = 4199.475 yard = 3.84 kms, approx 4 krosh = 1 yojana ≈ 9 miles ≈15 kms, approx
Prasna-Upanishad, Katho-Upanishad	Forms of Upanishad that encourages one to seek knowledge by questioning and through storytelling, respectively
Ramrajya	Rule of Ram
Sabha and Maha-sabha	Assembly hall. 'Maha' means 'Grand'
Samhita	Loosely translated as 'law'
Smarana	Memories, in Sanskrit
śyāma-ayas and Lohita-ayas	Iron is called śyāma ayas or śyāma alone. Copper is Lohāyasa

Term	Description
Tamil	The Iron-age name of language spoken widely in Southern India. The sanskrit name is 'Dramila'
vanavasa or vanaprastha	Denotes the 14 years that Rama, Sita and Lakshmana were in exile in forest
Vidha Peetam	Sanskrit term that means: Center of Learning
Places	
Andhra	The area traditionally lying between Godavari and Krishna Rivers
Anga	Also called as Vanga. Eastern kingdom in modern day Bengal
Aryavarta	The greater land of Aryan tribes
Asmaka	Bronze Age kingdom, west of Andhras, and in the Godavari belt
Ayodhya	Capital city of Raghu-vamsa lineage. Situated on the banks of River Sarayu
Bhima River	A tributary of Krishna river

Term	Description
Ch'in	Sanskrit word for China
Chandrakanti	City established by Chandraketu, son of Lakshmana
Chera or Cheralam	One of the traditional South Indian Kingdoms, approx. the area of mordern day state of Kerala. Finds mention in Vedas, Valmiki Ramayana etc.
Coramandel coast or *Karai-mandalam*	'Karai' in old Dravidian and modern Tamil means coast or bank. 'Mandalam' means a territory
Dakshin Bharat	South India
Danushkodi	Eastern-most tip of the land off Tamil country
Dhandak-Aranya	Dhandaka forest (or 'aranya') that stretched from Narmada river to Godavari/Krishna Rivers
Gandhara	One of the oldest Aryan kingdoms, in the present day Kandahar province of Afghanistan

Term	Description
Hariyupiya	Allegedly the Rig Vedic name for Harappa. This is disputed by some historians
Irawaddy River	Runs in modern day Myanmar, but finds mention in our puranas
Kalinga	Eastern kingdom in modern day Odisha
Kamboja	The land beyond Gandhara. Situated in North Eastern Iran bordering Afghanistan, traditionally believed as land of Pashtuns
Karupada	A place in Kalinga
Kashi	Modern day Varanasi. Vedic age city mentioned in all texts
Kekeya	Kingdom to which Kaikeyi, the third wife of Dasharatha belonged to. It was situated near Gandhara
Kemet	Ancient name for Egypt

Term	Description
Kishkinda	The land ruled by Vanar clan. This is believed to be based in and around modern day Hampi, but historians haven't conclusively proven that
Knossos	Also a Bronze Age civilization that ruled in the modern day island of Crete. Pre-dates the classical Greek (Mycanean civilization)
Konkan	The west coast of Chera country
Kosala	The kingdom from where Rama and his ancestors ruled from, with it's capital of Ayodhya
Krishna River	A river originating from the Western Ghats and flows through the Kishkinda and Andhras regions and joins Bay of Bengal (or Vanga ocean)
Kushavati	A city founded by Kush
Madhupura	Ancient name for Mathura, in UP state of India
Mahanadi River	Originates from the hills of Chattisgarh state and joins Bay of Bengal in the state of Odisha

Term	Description
Mahismati	Ancient capital of Chyavanas and was situated near to the modern-day city of Indore
Mahendragiri	A mountain bordering Pandya/Chera kingdom. Present day district of Tirunelveli
Maihar	A place in Madhya Pradesh, somewhere between Jabalpur and Varanasi
Malaya Rata province	A district in South-central Sri Lanka. This is believed to have been the base of Ravana.
Malwa	A district in Madhya Pradesh, with capital of what is now Indore/Ujjain. Supposedly the place where Lakshmana's son settled and established his own territory
Mount Ayomukha	ancient name for Mt. Rishyamukha, in Kishkinda, near modern day Hampi

Term	Description
Nile Aur	Old name for river Nile. 'Aur' is also how River is called in old Dravidian language, indicating some similarities and exchange with Indus valley and Dravidians
Onake Kindi	A small hamlet that has seen human settlements from Neolithic till late Iron Age. Situated on banks of River Tungabhadra, near modern day Hampi. A place where there are cave paintings depicting hunting scene dated to 1500 BCE
Pamban coast	Eastern-most strip of the land off Tamil country
Pampa River	Ancient name for River Tungabhadra, that is a tributary of Krishna river
Paudanyapura	Capital of Asmaka
Saketa	Another name for Ayodhya

Term	Description
Saraswati River	The legendary river that ran parallel to Indus river and is considered to have died due to natural calamities such as drought and earthquakes. This river too supported several cities and towns from the greater Indus valley civilization
Shravasti	City established by Luv, son of Rama, somewhere close to Ayodhya
Sone River	A tributary of Ganga river, and originates from modern day Chattisgarh state and joins Ganges near modern day Patna city
Sopara	A historical port in the Konkan territory, north of modern day Mumbai. This port subsequently went in decline, possibly due to changing coastal lines or possibly due to lack of patronage. Mentioned in several ancient texts as well as in foreign sources of Greeks, Arabs and Romans

Term	Description
Sumeria	One of the oldest civilization. The older name and smaller region of the land of Mesopotamia
Takshashila	City established by Taksha, who was the son of Bharata. In post Vedic times, this became a world renouned center of learning
Talaimannar	A town in the Northern-most tip of Sri Lanka
Vanga desa	Vanga is the old name for Bengal, the fertile delta land of Ganga and Brahmaputra rivers
Vidisha	One of the Aryavarta republics
People	
Ahar-Banas	Indus valley era people that settled in what is now Udaipur area. Banas is also name of a river in that region. This is also an Iron Age excavation site

Term	Description
Bharatas clan	One of the oldest clan after the legendary King Bharat, as mentioned in Rig Veda
Brahmin	A class of people, usually priests and scholars, that were placed at the top of the Vedic social hierarchy
Chandravanshi	The dynasty of kings associated with Moon
Chyavanas	a clan of Nagvanshis that lived in the Maihar area
Dasharajnas	Dasha - Ten; Rajnas - Rulers/Kings
Dravida	Traditionally referred to the lands south of Godavari. Modern archeological evidence suggests a close link with the Indus Valley/ Harappan Civilizational people, but this has not been conclusively proven
Elamites	People of Iran, with capital in Susa. Were known to have active trade with Indus Valley people
Hihaiyat	The clan that lived in upper Himalayan region

Term	Description
Hittite	Another Bronze Age civilization that ruled in the North Syrian/Iran/Turkey area. Rivals of Egyptian kingdom
Jahnus clan	An Aryan tribe to which Sita and King Janaka belong
Koitor tribe	A tribe that lives in present day Andhra/Chattisgarh/Orissa border areas.
Minoans	Another late Bronze age people in parts of Greece and Turkey
Mittani	A Bronze Age culture that ruled for several centuries in the Anatolian (Turkey) plateau
Mleccha	referrs in a crude way of barbaric foreign tribes
Mon–Kra	The people of Myanmar/Thailand
Mycenaens	A late Bronze Age Greek mainland civiilization
Nabateans	The name of people that lived in the Arabian peninsula

Term	Description
Naga	Literally means a Snake. Believe as deity of snakes worshipped from ancient times till date. Also represents the people said to have migrated from Myanmar/Thailand region in to North Eastern parts of India
Nagvanshi	The clan of Nagas
Pandya	One of the traditional South Indian Kingdoms, approx. the area of mordern day state of South Tamil Nadu. Finds mention in Vedas, Valmiki Ramayana etc.
Purus clan	One of the oldest clan as mentioned in Rig Veda. Led the warring tribes in a battle against King Sudas
Sakyas	One of the Aryan tribes, who settled in Lumbini. Around 6th BCE, this clan produced one of the most renouned sons - Siddartha Gautama. He is now popularly called as The Buddha.

Term	Description
Sea Peoples	A mysterious pirate-like people of whom little is known, but are recorded in various historical records of Egypt, Mittanis and Hittite. Their exact origin or who they were is still not resolved among historians
Shang people	Bronze Age Chinese civilization
Suryavanshi	The dynasty of kings associated with Surya
Turvasus clan	One of the ancient Aryan tribes to which Sage Durvasa belongs
Vanar clan	The clan to which Vali, Sugreeva and Hanuman belonged to. They ruled the Kishkinda kingdom
Yaksha and Yakshi	Group of people that were distinct from the Aryan tribes but were somewhat linked to them. At various points in mythology, the Yakshas either allied or fought against the Aryans

References

The following topics & related links are the material that I referred or read from which I drew inspiration to build the stories in my book:

Topic of reference	Reference Source
Valmiki's Ramayana	https://valmikiramayan.net/
Kambar's Ramavatharam	https://tinyurl.com/Kambar-Rama-English
Tulsidas' Sri Ramcharitmanas	http://www.gitapress.org/ BOOKS/1318/1318_Sri%20 Ramchritmanas_Roman.pdf
Valmiki Ramayana 'metre'	https://tinyurl.com/Valmiki-Ram-Anustubh-metre1 https://tinyurl.com/Valmiki-Ram-Anustubh-metre2

Topic of reference	Reference Source
Sugreeva's speech to his soldiers	Valmiki Ramayana, Kishkinda Kanda, Chapter 41
Ancient Measurement system of units	https://www.ijiras.com/2017/Vol_4-Issue_3/paper_24.pdf
Genetics (mtDNA) – Haplogroup R	https://en.wikipedia.org/wiki/Haplogroup_R_(mtDNA)
Inspired by Renuka Narayanan's article on Surpanaka	https://www.newindianexpress.com/opinions/2024/May/12/the-most-beloved-villain-among-indian-epics Indian Express, 13th May 2024
Battle of Qadesh, 1275 BCE	https://en.wikipedia.org/wiki/Battle_of_Kadesh
Battle of Djahy, 1178 BCE	https://en.wikipedia.org/wiki/Battle_of_Djahy

Topic of reference	Reference Source
Weapons & Tools found in Tamil Nadu with Harappan/Indus script	http://www.hinduonnet.com/2006/05/01/stories/2006050101992000.htm
Mittanis, Hittite, Akkadians, Egyptians + Gods of Mittani	https://www.worldhistory.org/Mitanni/
Aadu-puli-aattam (Goats & Tigers) board game	https://www.traditionalgames.in/aadu-puli-attam-atu-puli-attam/
Bibek Debroy's translation of Ramayana	https://archive.org/details/valmikiramayance/page/n23/mode/2up
Battle of Dasharajnas in Rigveda + King Sudas	https://tinyurl.com/Rig-Veda-Sudas

Topic of reference	Reference Source
Inspiration for Part 3 (Sitamma Mayamma)	Sammakka Saralamma Jathara or Medaram Jathara is a koya tribal festival that originated in 13th CE, but is still prevalent in state of Telengana. https://www.medaramjathara.com/
Seals of Muwatalli-II	https://tinyurl.com/Muwatalli-Seals
Human mtDNA Haplogroup R in India	Thesis by Monika Karmin, University of Tartu
Koya / Koitor Tribe of India	Handbook on "Koya," by Prof.(Dr.)A.B. Ota, Director, Shri T. Sahoo, O.S.D., 2015; Bhubaneswar, Odisha state.
IRON AGE – ANTIQUITY OF IRON IN INDIA	Ravi Korisettar and Smitha S Kumar http://archaeologyonline.net/artifacts/iron-ore

Topic of reference	Reference Source
Harappa script & Evidence of seals in Ahar-Banas culture, 3500 years ago	Prof. S. Kalyanaraman https://tinyurl.com/SKal-Ahar-Banas-Script https://tinyurl.com/SKal-Ahar-Banas-Seals
Legend of Parashurama	https://www.indiadivine.org/parashurama-6th-avatar-lord-vishnu/
Maps	Where possible, I have drawn some maps and schemas for visual representation; In other instances, I have used existing map outlines from sources that are cited in the map itself.